# Things We Do Not Tell The People We Love

Huma Qureshi is an award-winning writer, and former *Observer* and *Guardian* reporter. Her memoir *How We Met: A Memoir of Love and Other Misadventures* was published in January 2021 by Elliott & Thompson, to critical acclaim, chosen by *Stylist* as one of 2021's best non-fiction. She is the winner of the 2020 *Harper's Bazaar* Short Story Prize. She lives in London.

*Huma Qureshi*

# Things We Do Not Tell The People We Love

SCEPTRE

First published in Great Britain in 2021 by Sceptre
An Imprint of Hodder & Stoughton
An Hachette UK company

1

A CIP catalogue record for this title is available from the British Library

Hardback ISBN 9781529368673
eBook ISBN 9781529368680

Typeset in Monotype Bembo by Manipal Technologies Limited

Printed and bound in Great Britain by Clays Ltd, Elcograf S.p.A.

Hodder & Stoughton policy is to use papers that are natural, renewable and recyclable
products and made from wood grown in sustainable forests. The logging and
manufacturing processes are expected to conform to the environmental regulations of
the country of origin.

Hodder & Stoughton Ltd
Carmelite House
50 Victoria Embankment
London EC4Y 0DZ

www.sceptrebooks.co.uk

*For Richard*

# Contents

Premonition                                1

Summer                                    23

Firecracker                               43

The Jam Maker                             59

Superstitious                             75

Foreign Parts                             89

Too Much                                  97

Waterlogged                              129

Small Differences                        151

The Wishes                               167

'I wanted to go to where the crying was, and I continued to climb the stairs between the black, wide-open windows. I finally came to where the crying was, behind a white door. I went in, felt her close to me and turned on the light.

But I saw no one in the room, and heard nothing more. And yet there, on the sofa, was the handkerchief, damp with her tears.'

– Elio Vittorini, *Name and Tears*

# Premonition

My mother had mentioned offhand to me that you were engaged to be married to a girl who had studied medicine at Oxford and I had thought, *but of course*. I remembered how exceptionally picky your mother was about these things. I had been on my way to meet Cameron at the time so I was not paying much attention to what my mother was saying and was in a rush to end our call but after I had caught my breath from running for the bus, I remember thinking it was not so surprising that you had ended up following convention and doing things so traditionally after all.

I had little reason to think about you or your wedding again until Cameron's birthday several months later when we went out for dinner at Mildreds. It had been raining thickly and we squeezed through the door to join the back of a huddle of warm bodies waiting for tables, everyone's coats smelling like bonfires and damp leaves. Cameron turned to kiss me and as he leaned in, I thought I saw you behind him, standing in line next to a girl with a head full of tight curls golden at the tips. I couldn't be sure, for it had easily been ten years or perhaps even more since I had seen you, but I recognised something. It was there in the way that you stood slightly slouched and in your face, which had not changed so much. I must have been staring at you because when Cameron moved away again, he squeezed my hand and laughed, 'Hey, who are you checking out on my birthday?'

When we moved to our table and sat down, I stole a better look. Shadows flickered across your face from the low-hanging copper lights and perhaps you had that odd feeling of being watched, for you looked up right then and caught my eye. And that's when I realised it really was you, because that was exactly what we used to do.

*

I had first felt you looking at me when I was fifteen years old. We had known each other as children, which is to say we did not know each other at all. Our parents had been friends since before we were even born but you and I barely spoke to each other. Though my mother had told me once that we played together at each other's houses when we were very small – something I certainly did not and still do not remember – by the time we reached secondary school certain lines had been drawn and I understood that I was not supposed to talk to boys and it was, I imagine, the same for you with girls. But then you started looking at me.

The first time it happened, we were at a dinner party at an uncle and aunty's house, or so we called them though they were not blood relatives, but just another Pakistani family we happened to know. All of our parents did this back then: hosted dinners for sixty or seventy people at a time, squeezing more guests than they could comfortably accommodate into each other's houses every single Saturday night. Back then the English girls from my girls' school went to real parties, teenage house parties with boys and alcohol and no parents at all, and it embarrassed me how boring my life was. Our dinner parties were our parents' idea of a good time. They loved these parties; they lived for these Saturday nights, when all the men, all the fathers, sat around on long sofas discussing politics and the state of the NHS, in which they all happened to work, uninterrupted, while the women, our mothers, helped each other in the kitchen and laid dining tables and stacked paper plates with bought-in-bulk napkins, gossiping. Actually, perhaps that is unfair; to this day, I have no idea what our mothers talked about, but I can guess now that some of it might have been about the lives they had left behind to make this country their home.

Meanwhile, we sat upstairs in separate bedrooms, girls in one, boys in another. All of us girls sat on the floor watching films while you boys were across the hallway fighting over computer games or football. Like the other girls, I had to dress up for these dinners in fancy silk shalwar kameez, brightly coloured and embroidered but mostly badly-fitting outfits that smelt like the suitcases in the loft and which I hated because they made me feel like a Christmas tree, but you got away with just tee-shirts and jeans. It bothered me that none of the boys were required to make an effort, that our mothers didn't collectively look you all up and down and scrutinise you the way they did us, assessing the fairness of our skin, the curve of our pubescent waists, the early signs of our marriageability.

Sometimes, the older girls whispered about crushes they weren't supposed to have. They talked about you especially, because you were considered the best-looking one, with unusually creamy skin, gold-flecked hair and deep-set chestnut eyes. I admit this was a novelty for all of us. 'He doesn't even look Pakistani,' they used to say, awestruck, in spite of your scruffy clothes. I had heard the other boys sneer at you and call you pretty, because you were also very skinny in a runner's sort of way, but you just laughed and shrugged it off like the rock star we all thought you were.

That first time I felt it – your eyes upon me – we'd been summoned to the dining room for dinner. It was customary to call the children down for food after our fathers had been served but before our mothers, and we would help ourselves to paper plates that dented in the middle under the combined weight of rice, chicken and shop-bought pizza brought out especially for us kids, and which we carried back carefully to our designated rooms, the bedroom carpets protected from potential spills with crisp white sheets sellotaped to the skirting boards. At this particular house, the dining table had been pushed back against the wall to make space for the guests and we were ushered in by some of the aunties, queued as though we were at an all-you-can-eat buffet. But you stood out of line, slouching against a sideboard, clutching a paper plate to your chest. You always had this attitude about you that seemed to say you were better than all of this and I liked that, because inside I sort of felt the same way too. I saw you from the corner of my eye, stood there, and all of a sudden, I realised you were watching me, even though there were other people around. I don't remember how I knew, only that I felt it, only that I could sense I was being watched because my skin tickled and I became aware of my own breathing. When I realised it was you watching me, somewhere inside of me a series of synapses sparked. I looked up then, shy and unsure, and though I caught your eye and though we both looked away again, it was not before you held my gaze just a fraction longer than was appropriate.

Later that night you were all I could think of and yet I'd never even spoken to you in my entire life.

\*

It went on for months, at every Saturday-night dinner we went to: a private symphony of glances that varied in intensity, movement and pace. It made me uneasy but not in an altogether unpleasant way; I felt brighter, prettier, stranger, by which I mean closer to unique, under the hold of your gaze. I quickly understood, of course, that this was something that was just between us, something only we did, something we didn't need to talk to anyone else about and certainly not to each other. It was our secret. But still, sometimes, I convinced myself I was imagining it because you were older than me and the best-looking of all the boys and there were plenty of prettier girls with long shiny dark hair in our group for you to consider. I was thin and flat-chested, quiet and bookish, short and bespectacled. I played the piano and this was the only thing I could think of that made me different. You knew this because my parents always made me play for our guests when dinners were held at our house. But apart from that, there was little reason for me to stand out. There was no logical explanation for your interest in me.

*

I began to feel you like some kind of premonition. Somehow you appeared at the same time I did across landings and in hallways and dining rooms, as though you were waiting for me, as though you knew I'd be there. You'd hold my gaze; I'd look away but when I looked back, there you were again. It progressed. We'd pass each other on the stairs, me going up, you coming down, and in the space between heartbeats you'd brush my hand or my arm, once or twice even the small of my back as you followed me, and I knew it was intentional because it kept happening. Your touches were tiny, seemingly accidental – sometimes your fingers pressing the tips of mine as you wordlessly passed me a glass or a plate – but they cracked me open, like lightning across the sky. Our star-crossed moments may have lasted only milliseconds, but they filled the whole of my small schoolgirl world and kept it turning, like shafts of dust dancing gold in a splinter of sunlight.

Though once I was bored by them, now I could no longer wait for Saturday nights. They always seemed so far away. The weeks passed slowly; I used to spend every break time desperately trying to catch snatches of what the other girls at school were saying, making mental notes on their conversation so that one day I might have been able to join in, but now I preferred being on my own because it gave me time to think of you. I'd sit in a stairwell with my Walkman and I'd replay our latest exchange of secret looks to a soundtrack of love songs and every beat made my heart ache because I yearned for you. I began to care more about my appearance, begging my mother to let me swap my glasses for contacts and pluck my eyebrows, asking her to alter my shalwar kameez – the only clothes you ever saw me in – so that they might be slightly more flattering and she humoured me, I guess, because she thought it meant I was interested in my roots or something. But all I wanted was to find a way to keep you looking at me, to not have you drop your gaze or swap your attention to someone else.

When Saturday evenings finally came around, I searched for clues to find out whether your family had already arrived at whosoever's house we were invited to next, scanning the long line of cars parked all the way down to the end of the road looking for yours, seeking for a glimpse of your trainers in the rubble of guests' shoes discarded untidily in heaps by the front door. Sometimes you weren't there and on those nights I felt my heart sink. On the drive home I would slump, sullen in response to my parents when they asked if I had fun.

I found dinner parties at your house especially thrilling, overwhelmed by the notion that I was right there, in the place where you lived and dreamed and breathed, knowing that my hands might pass where yours had already been. Every little thing inside your house took on meaning; sipping from a glass, I found myself wondering if perhaps you'd drunk from the same one, washed it yourself and left it on the draining board, and this alone left me feeling lightheaded. More than once I slipped inside your bedroom without anyone knowing while you boys watched the football in your TV lounge. I remember your room smelt like musk or warm bodies or clothes left out too long in pale rain, a smell that later at university I came to know was what the inside of most boys' bedrooms smelt like, and the crevices of their skin first thing in the morning. But I was an only child so back then this was all still a mystery to me. The sight of your bed sheets crumpled made my head spin though I did not fully understand why. I never stayed long but I caught glimpses of your books by writers whom I did not yet know like Solzhenitsyn and Sartre, and I sifted through your CDs, surprised to find you liked the same sort of music my father kept on twelve-inch. The Carpenters, Cat Stevens, Lou Reed. I began to search for you in the lyrics of my father's songs, repeating them in my head. *Hello my love, I heard a kiss from you.* Sometimes I thought about taking something, a book, perhaps a paper from your desk covered by your handwriting, just to have something that belonged to you, but in my awkward shalwar kameez I had no pockets to put things in.

*

At Mildreds I made no conscious effort to look at you but I felt you there like a faint shadow, glancing across at me while I laughed with Cameron or covered his hand with mine or when he lifted his spoon to my mouth so I might taste his dessert. While once I might have cared that someone from the small place where I grew up, which now felt a million miles away, had seen me with Cameron, it had stopped bothering me a long time ago. When my mother asked where I was or who I was with, I was not completely forthright and spared her the finer details but at least I did not lie about it completely or pretend that Cameron did not exist. She knew his name, had deduced herself, I think, through a process of elimination that I was more or less living with him. But for all it might have pained her, she had not yet confronted me about it so I took her silence as a sort of begrudging acceptance after all these years. Though I did not bring him up unless she asked, I was done with the secrets and the lies. I had spent my life at university living like that, hiding boyfriends like crumpled love letters, and now I was too old for it. I briefly wondered who the girl you were having dinner with was, the gorgeous girl with the tight gold-tipped Afro curls whose wine you poured and whose hand you held. She was obviously not the good Pakistani girl who had studied medicine at Oxford and thus not the girl your family had proudly announced you were engaged to.

Cameron had left the table for the bathroom and I was shrugging on my coat, still damp and nubby from the rain, when our eyes locked again. You nodded in my direction by way of acknowledgement, as if the years that had passed hung there suspended in the fine particles of air. The girl you were with was looking down at her phone, her features illuminated softly by the glow, ethereal. When he returned, I let Cameron guide me to the door and as we walked past outside

I could just about see you, hazy and unclear through the mist of shadowy condensation that had gathered on the inside.

*

I was seventeen when it finally happened.

With the passing of time in a place that perhaps now felt like home, our parents had learnt to be more relaxed and had settled, like perennials in soft soil. There were still rules but at Saturday-night dinners, us girls and you boys were no longer quite as segregated any more. I suppose our parents had come to understand that it was only a matter of time and that we would eventually mix. I guess some even saw it as a good thing, in the anticipation of marriages one day being arranged. It was a gradual change, small concessions, but, for us teenagers, mostly it meant we could sit in the same room.

We were never completely on our own but we could talk at least a little bit now, which was better than not talking at all. The first time you ever spoke to me, you smiled and said something like how you wished you'd had the chance to learn how to play the piano and in that split second I felt dizzy because of the sound of your voice, the words accompanying your eyes that looked straight into mine. My head was already full of you by this point, but when we began to talk it overflowed. Each time we spoke, even if it was just in passing in a doorway, I half held my breath and I could feel my heart thumping somewhere in my chest because though your words said one thing, your eyes said something else deeper. In time, we sought each other out at our parents' dinner parties in subtle ways that seemed accidental, milling around in the same side of whichever room we'd been designated to so that we might talk for twenty minutes or so. We were careful not to stay too long in each other's company, knowing instinctively that it would make others talk, but we always found a way to come back to each other, to pick up the thread of our conversation; a chat over dessert, another out in the hallway if we happened to accidentally pass each other. At first we talked only about things like movies and books, school and subject choices, but none of it felt trivial and all of it made me fall for you more and more. In time, as months passed, we began to confide in each other about how we both longed to escape this small town and every word you said crept under my skin and stayed there. Some nights, I dreamed of us escaping together. Sometimes at parties at your house, a bunch of us would sit in your room and you'd play us your favourite records and you'd look over at me and smile and every time I felt like you'd picked each song for me, my heart turning like a cartwheel. Once at my house, you hung back by my piano and I tried to teach you a concerto, even going so far as to place your fingers softly on the keys when no one was looking, while inside my stomach flipped and I could barely breathe. Touching your hand, no matter how lightly, was the most daring thing I'd ever done. I still did not know much about boys, anything in fact, in any physical, real sort of way but the only thing I understood was that I longed for you with an ache that tugged at me inside, two hands not wanting to let go for fear of falling.

*

When it finally happened, I was seventeen. It was a blazing summer's day, the sky blue and clear, broken only by threads of thin clouds and white butterflies floating like bits of ripped paper in a breeze. It was the summer before you were to leave for university, which was something I did not want to have to think about. You planned to study law in Edinburgh and the distance seemed unfathomable to me, as though you were flying off into your own unknown galaxy – but your parents had made it clear they expected you home often, and so I took some solace in that.

On that day we had been invited to a barbecue at the home of an uncle and auntie who were both doctors, not just the uncle. As we pulled up on the road outside their large, symmetrical three-storey house, the driveway already crowded with cars, my father pointed out to my mother, who did not work, that this was the difference a wife with an extra income made. They had one son, with whom you were good friends; not just from the dinner parties – he went to your boys' school. I didn't know him but I didn't like the way you changed into someone less intelligent whenever he was around – jostling in pretend fights, rugby-tackling each other on the stairs, only ever talking about football.

When I arrived with my parents, most people were already outside in the tremendous garden, which was about the size of a small park. The air was smoky, heavy from chunks of marinated meat left upon the grill, but there was a sweetness drifting too, nestled by the clusters of white roses and jasmine, under the honeysuckle trailing along the fence. I spotted you on the patio behind a trestle table covered with a white paper tablecloth, helping pour drinks. I walked over and you smiled sideways and murmured, 'Listen, come with me,' and so of course, I did. Nobody noticed us go indoors.

I could sense what was going to happen the same way I somehow knew beforehand if I'd passed an exam or the way I still know if the landline might ring and who might be on the other end. But even so, I held my breath in one long inhale because to exhale would be to let the possibility go. I didn't stop to think about it because if I did, I would have walked straight back outside again. No matter how much I wanted it, my upbringing had taught me this was wrong. We both knew that. But still I followed you, first inside and then up the stairs. You didn't look behind, trusting only that I was there. When we crossed the first floor you reached your hand out behind you. At first, just the tips of our fingers touched but then as we crossed the second floor, our fingers laced lightly, and I remember thinking how your hands were just so lovely; I remember finding it hard to breathe, the thrill too much to bear.

Neither of us said a word. We reached the third floor and entered a bedroom under the eaves. I noticed the football team posters on the wall and the piles of clothes thrown messily on the floor and I realised that this was your friend's bedroom. It was painted a frosty light blue, as though we were up in the coldest part of the sky. The skylight was shut and the room smelt moist, like sweat. When you turned and shut the door your eyes finally found mine again and my heart spun round and round, like a paper windmill.

Your face was so close to mine, I could feel you breathing through your nose. You touched the side of my face softly and my heart quickened. You closed your eyes. I kept mine open. You leaned in and you were so close, your face was blurry. Your lips felt like ice upon mine, at first dry little nibbles, which was not at all how I had imagined it would be. But then you carried on deeper and it was only when your hands stroked my collarbone and then tugged at the neckline of my kameez, the expression on your face strange now, that I changed my mind, and my conviction, that I must have wanted this, gave way.

Your hands held my throat firm not because you wanted to hurt me, I think, but because you wanted me to stay, holding me in place up against the door. I turned my head and I bit my lip but you kept at it, ravenous. 'Hang on, don't,' I whispered but your eyes were still shut and you were still lost some place far away. I didn't want to say anything any louder in case someone else might hear; I couldn't risk anyone walking in. So I said nothing because I realised then that even if I did, you wouldn't listen anyway and so then I let you do whatever you wanted to.

It was only a kiss – or rather, a complicated series of terribly bad ones, accompanied by some stilted attempts to touch me through my clothes – but I, like you, had been brought up with an innocence and a sense of obligation that had led me to believe that even a kiss was to be saved for after marriage. My throat hurt where your hands had been (though your fingers had seemed gentle, they were stronger than I thought they would be) and rather than a surge of something wondrous, I felt shaken, as though you had taken something from me. But more than that, I felt as though I must have done something wrong. At some point you let me go but before you left the room, while I straightened my clothes, I scratched my head and asked 'Why?' and you looked puzzled before you shrugged and replied that I had given you the impression that it was okay. I thought you must have been right because I had, after all, crossed these lines myself, talking to you for longer than I should have done, daring to take your hand and place your fingers on the keys of my piano, looking back at you into your chestnut eyes; dreaming of you at night.

At university, by which time I had long ago left you and this small waterlogged world far behind, there were occasional nights when I'd find myself in somebody else's bed. I'd whisper, 'Hang on, don't,' or sometimes just, 'Please stop.' Afterwards I'd lie still in the dark, my body throbbing from being pushed and held by somebody else's ungentle hands, and I'd wonder how I even came to be there. Once or twice, I remembered what you had said, how I gave off the impression that it was okay. That I'd asked for it, in a way.

*

When I saw your name in my inbox a fortnight after Mildreds, it felt inevitable, the same way I can tell if a piece of news will be bad or good. Though I had not specifically thought about you in any concerted, deliberate way, I had still somehow half-expected to hear from you. I was not surprised you had managed to track me down. Your message was formal and brief. 'Hi,' you wrote. 'We saw each other a few weekends ago. I'd like to catch up. Shall we meet?' In your presumptuousness, you suggested a time and a place.

I didn't reply but then you wrote again on the day you had suggested to say that you would be there in any case. I ignored your message until about an hour before I was due to leave. 'Okay,' I typed. 'See you there.'

We met in a nondescript coffee shop by the back entrance of Liverpool Street Station, the sort of place that didn't see daylight and had dirty floors and served thin black coffee and dry croissants days old. I thought you could have at least chosen a nicer place. You had come from work, or so I assumed, and were already waiting for me in a booth, a black coat over your suit. Seeing you here under the glum reality of cold strip lighting, it struck me how astonishingly old you were. I had not noticed this in Mildreds. Here there were dull blue shadows under your eyes, patches of dry skin visible at your temples. You used to be so handsome, so attractive. I wondered briefly how I might have looked to you.

'Hi,' you said. 'Can I get you a drink?'

I said no.

'It's been a while.' You laughed, a nervous twitch.

'Indeed,' I said, and I noticed how, now, you could not look me in the eye. 'So, this is all out of the blue. What was it you wanted to meet for?' I asked.

You scratched the side of your head and then you sighed and said that it was awkward. 'Here's the thing,' you explained. The girl you were out for dinner with in Mildreds was a close friend, but you were aware it might have looked like something else. You weren't sure if I knew, you continued, but you were engaged now and it would make things difficult if anyone were to misunderstand, if the news of you being out for dinner with someone else, even if only a female friend, somehow made it back to your parents.

I coughed, stifled a laugh. Honestly, I thought, because even in what little I had observed of the way you both were, it was so obvious she was more than just some female friend. But instead I told you that it didn't bother me, that it was none of my business anyway. In a way, I was almost flattered that you thought me important enough to have to explain but at the same time, I felt sorry for you that you cared so much about appearances sake, just like everyone else. Then for some reason I added that I had a boyfriend, as if that explained something. Neither of us said anything for a moment and I wished that I had said yes to a coffee, if only to have given my hands something to hold.

'Thank you,' you said after a pause. And then, 'Listen, I know some strange shit happened between us when we were young. I don't remember how it all turned out so, you know, badly.'

'Don't worry about it,' I said. 'It was a lifetime ago.' There was nothing much else to say then, so I made my excuses and left. I saw you leave the coffee shop from the corner of my eye, aware of the shape of you turning the opposite direction to take the Central line. When I looked across, you had already disappeared into the blurred crowds swelling down into the tunnels.

*

After what happened in your friend's bedroom, we didn't have the chance to speak. I thought about you a lot but it wasn't accompanied by my usual ache of yearning. I was distracted, spent a lot of time leaving books half-finished, staring into space. Then the A level results came out and you had done well, your proud parents phoning mine with the news. I knew my parents would write you a cheque and fold it crisply inside a card and that we would go around to your house to congratulate you and your parents in person. I thought I might have seen you then, but before I knew it you had left for Edinburgh and instead of visiting your house, my mother mailed your card with the cheque tucked inside to your parents' address. It was a time before we had phones of our own and though I thought about asking Uncle, your father, for your university email address under the pretence of seeking advice for my UCAS form, I changed my mind. So I had no way of talking to you but a part of me was relieved. I didn't know what I might have said in any case.

A few months later I found my mother sitting at the dining table with her head in her hands. I rushed to her but she looked up at me with angry eyes and asked, 'How could you?'

It unfolded that you had told your friend, the one whose bedroom we had been in, about how we had gone up to his room, along with a highly embellished and inaccurate account of what had happened in there.

Your friend had told other boys, other sons of people our parents knew, and somehow one of their mothers, one of the aunties, had overheard. She demanded her son tell her everything he knew. She in turn called your mother and then mine and then all hell broke loose.

For months afterwards, our scandal was all that was talked about. I don't know what happened when you came home from Edinburgh or what you said to your parents or how you explained it away, because until that night in Mildreds, I never saw you again. The story I heard was that it was me who had asked you to come upstairs and that we had lain tangled upon your friend's bed, not that you had me pinned up against the door, and you can see how, clearly, this made things worse.

My parents avoided Saturday-night dinners for a year until it all more or less blew over, although to this day it has never been fully forgotten. For a long time my father left the room whenever I came in, while my mother was more vocal about her disappointment in me. I am grateful we have since discovered we both prefer silence to shouting. Soon enough I escaped to university. From what I understand, your mother remained furious at mine for many years, reminding her often that our family was beneath yours. She said that when the time would eventually come, they would not accept anything less than a respectable, well-edu-cated, professional, modest girl from an outstanding family for you, the implication being of course that I was anything but and that you, you were perfect.

*

I have never told Cameron about any of this because it was so long ago, because it doesn't matter, because it is absurd that all of this happened over an unfortunate teenage kiss. In some lights, it is ridiculous, truly it is, and so it has not occurred to me that this story might be a defining feature of my life, an important enough thing to tell the person I love.

But sometimes it makes me so incredibly sad to remember how this episode in my life made me feel; the bad, guilty girl. Sometimes when I read depressing news I think about how unfair the world can be and this dark feeling creeps over me like a fog. Times like these I run as fast as I can. I don't think about you particularly but there are times when I have been alone at dawn, running by the river in the sharp chill of a cruel cold morning when for some reason I am reminded of the feeling of hands at my throat and I stop, startled and breathless, because (and I don't know why) it feels as though my chest might split in two. But I have learnt that stopping only makes it hurt harder and the only thing to do is to push through and so I sprint on faster, chasing the whispers away. I suppose in some ways perhaps all of this does matter. Or it does and it doesn't. I haven't exactly figured it all out.

# *Summer*

A month ago, Reem had invited her mother on holiday to the south of France without necessarily thinking it through or speaking to Anthony about it first. Ever since then, Reem had been trying to convince herself that having her mother on holiday with them wouldn't be so bad. As Anthony had pointed out, she could look after the children; perhaps they could finally have some time to themselves. But now, days before they were due to leave, Reem stared at her suitcase wondering what clothes to pack that wouldn't provoke a fight with her mother, who was strict about things like modesty and not wearing tops without sleeves, and realised that inviting her mother on holiday was in fact a huge mistake and that, if she was honest with herself, she had known this all along.

They would be away for seven days under the swell of the heat and Reem felt the uneasiness creeping around the edges of her skin already. She threw her favourite vintage denim shorts on the floor. 'Some fucking holiday this'll be,' she said, walking out and slamming the bedroom door.

The day her mother called, the day Reem accidentally ended up inviting her on holiday, her mother had sounded shrunken on the phone. She often did.

She lived in Cheshire, a five-hour train ride away from Reem and Anthony, who had moved from Clapham to Brighton when Sami was born. If she was honest, the distance served Reem well. Their conversations were often brief, broken by one small child or the other pulling at Reem's leg, demanding her attention. Reem was grateful for these interruptions because the longer she spoke to her mother, the more likely it was that they would fall out over one thing or the other. It had always been that way.

It was not that Reem did not care about her mother exactly, but sometimes she didn't know what to say, aware that her life was full to the seams with small children and the chaos and colour of family life in a way that her mother's life was not. Moments before Reem invited her mother to France, her mother muttered again how long it had been since she had seen her grandchildren and Reem could picture the corners of her thin mouth turned down in complaint. 'You are always so busy,' she said. 'I never see you any more.' More than once, her mother had said something along the lines of how she had given up so much to raise Reem, surely Reem could give something up for her too. This sort of thing happened every so often when they had been speaking too frequently or for too long, resentment tinting every word they exchanged like the threat of grey rain in cold spring. When she was younger Reem used to retaliate, raising her voice and pointing out the absurdity and the unfairness of whatever it was her mother might have been saying, but since having children of her own she no longer had the energy.

On this occasion, she just sighed. Reem had that morning paid the deposit for their holiday villa that happened to have an extra bedroom and it was then that she asked her mother if she wanted to join them. The words formed themselves like the bubbles of speech that appeared in Sami's cartoons and Lila's picture books and Reem did not quite realise what she had said until a second afterwards, her words hanging in the air then popping away one by one as her mother accepted. The truth was Reem was tired of her mother making her feel guilty and she had wanted in a rush to find a way to shut her up, to prove to her momentarily that she was not such a thoughtless or selfish daughter after all.

*

It was a sign of Anthony's patience that he did not particularly mind that his mother-in-law would be joining them on their family holiday, even though it was not something he would have ever suggested himself, knowing how difficult the relationship between Reem and her mother could be. But by the night before their flight, Anthony's reassurance that everything would be fine had turned to indifference.

She sat sullen after dinner, playing with her cutlery. 'You know what she's like. One day it'll be fine and then the next, I'll have done something wrong. We've spent a fortune on this place with a pool and I won't even be able to wear my goddamn swimsuit. What have I done?' she said. Anthony picked up her plate and then wiped the table beneath it.

'Well, you were the one who asked her to come with us.' He shrugged, bored of the conversation, and for a second Reem felt like picking up her knife and stabbing him in the thigh. She dropped it on the floor instead, pretending it was an accident. Anthony bent down to pick it up and rolled his eyes.

Reem had tried to tell Anthony in the past what it was like for her growing up and though he shook his head softly in sympathy, she knew he could never completely understand, and this hurt her so much, it stung her eyes. Her upbringing had been left to her mother. Her father was a man she barely knew who, from her birth right up until his death, worked for nine months of every year overseas in the oil industry in the Middle East. 'It wasn't just about the clothes,' she had tried to explain but then she struggled to express the void she felt because there was no single point of drama that she could refer to in order to make some sense of it all, no individual trauma that had left her crudely damaged or explained why things were the way they were. It was as though something between them had always been broken, that was all. Sometimes Reem wondered if she had imagined it, because it was only little things, she told herself. But it was lots of little things, too many to count, and together they added up to something immense. In the end it was the little things she could not forget. Reem had come to realise that whatever it was that was sour between them had always been there, ever since she was a child; a low discord of misplaced frequency humming between them like a lullaby, only off-key.

When Reem was a little girl, her mother used to yank crossly at her tee-shirts whenever they accidentally rode up to reveal a sliver of her tea-coloured stomach. She forbade Reem as a teenager from wearing leggings on the premise that Lycra clung too tight and revealed the curve of Reem's calves and thighs to boys and men who liked to look. 'Cover your buttocks,' she reproved, and it made Reem shudder to hear her mother say such an ugly word out loud. When Reem came home from her first term of university, her mother discovered a black halter-neck in a bag of laundry. Reem had worn it out dancing a few nights before. A boy from her practical advocacy seminar had come up behind her, kissing her left shoulder, his lips moving lightly across her skin, his warm fingers lifting her hair to reach the tender dip at the base of her neck as they swayed to R&B. Reem had forgotten she had dropped the top in with the rest of her dirty clothes and pretended it belonged to her best friend Imogen, but her mother was quick and untrusting, and for the rest of the holidays Reem had to surrender her mobile phone while her mother checked it for further evidence of miscreance.

Reem grew stealthy, hiding photos of parties and notes from boys who fell in love with her safely inside a series of heavy textbooks, setting a password on her laptop and phone, giving her more revealing outfits to Imogen to borrow and keep safe over the long holidays. She ignored most of her mother's calls, which came several times a day, even though it made things worse when eventually they did speak. The summer before her final year, she told her mother she needed to go back to university for some extra reading in the library but she took the train to London to spend a day with a boy from her halls instead, kissing him for hours under a secluded tree in Regent's Park. A part of her found it thrilling, keeping secrets like this, but sometimes she wondered if it made her as selfish, as bad, as her mother had always said she was.

Reem had wished for a mother like Imogen's, the sort of mother whom her friends could call casually by her first name, who might have talked to her about things like feminism over a home-cooked breakfast after a late night out and always paid her compliments. 'But I'm your mother. It's my job to point out your flaws,' was something Reem's mother liked to say. 'I have to tell you about them so that you might improve yourself, because no one else will.' Years later her mother had tried to talk her out of marrying Anthony, shouting not just that Reem had shamed her but that he would leave her because that was what English men did. In the end she accepted it only because Reem said in anger that if she had to choose between them, she would, and that also, to all intents and purposes, didn't her own father leave them both anyway, even when he was alive? At this point her mother gave up, presumably realising it was preferable to retain some contact with Reem rather than lose her completely, which would have been even more difficult to explain to those who might have asked.

Reem had read long ago in a women's magazine that relationships between mothers and adult daughters largely improved with pregnancy and a part of her imagined this might happen when she was expecting Sami. She read stories of hard mothers, toxic, the articles called them, who softened like scoops of ice cream in the sun the very moment they became grandmothers. But Reem and her mother still fought, first over small things like the choice of Sami's name and then over bigger things too. When Reem said that they would not shave his soft newborn head, her mother refused to speak to her for months. By the time Lila was born, Reem busier now with two small children and the move to Brighton, it became easier to use the children as an excuse and allow the thin fraying thread between them to slacken. Reem had often felt her mother was a world away and, after her father's death particularly, she had grown to understand that there was nothing much between them but empty space, an air crowded with millions of misunderstandings.

*

Reem saw her mother waiting by the check-in desk where they had agreed to meet. Her mother looked tidy, like a neat parcel, wearing spotless white trainers, navy jogging bottoms and a striped navy and white long-sleeved top, her hair tied back in a small low bun. A beige cardigan was folded over one arm and a small brown suitcase stood by her side. It had been six months since Reem had last seen her, when they had thrown a small fourth birthday party at home for Sami and her mother had stayed for the weekend. They had quarrelled then too, over a throwaway remark her mother had made about Sami preferring his other grandmother to her, suggesting it was Reem's doing. 'Do you blame him, though?' Reem had said, her face burning. Standing in the airport now her mother looked so much older than she had then, so small and harmless, Reem thought, and in that tiny moment her throat cracked as a breath escaped and she felt overcome and a little ashamed.

Her mother turned. Reem waved. She pointed in her mother's direction and said, 'Look, Nani's here.' Her mother knelt down slowly with her arms wide and outstretched as Sami and Lila ran towards her. Her mother's face though tired was soft and she glowed as she held Sami and Lila close to her and kissed their small pink faces again and again. They jumped up at her like puppies. Reem felt a stab of guilt again just then, for the distance she kept between them. Anthony looked over at Reem and said, 'Hey, come on. We'll have a great time. Look how happy they are, see?' and Reem nodded as she dragged one of their suitcases behind her.

On the flight Sami and Lila sat on either side of her mother in a row of three. 'Are you sure, Ma?' Reem asked, having planned to sit between the children herself. Lila, who was three, was still clingy and sometimes cried only for Reem, pushing even Anthony away. But her mother waved Anthony and Reem off to their own seats, three aisles behind. 'You two have a break,' she said. 'I will take care of them.' Her mother had come prepared with a magazine each for the children covered with their favourite characters from TV shows and a small tin box of lemon drops to keep their ears from popping at take-off. 'Thank you, Ma,' Reem said and she felt she meant it, too.

It was often like this. For the first few hours of every visit, Reem convinced herself that their relationship was never quite as bad as it felt in her head. Every time, for those first few hours of being back together again, she pictured putting their past behind her, sending her mother flowers and surprising her with trips to the theatre, booking a mother and daughter visit to some luxury spa. From her window seat, she could see the top of her mother's small, dark head turning from child to child and she could just about hear her voice softly cajoling them. Just then she felt terrible for thinking her mother was so awful, just as she did every time her mother sent the children presents in the post or she saw the excited looks upon her children's faces when they heard Nani was coming to stay. She thought about the impression other people had of her mother; a small, sweet, devoted grandmother who lived too far away from her only child and grandchildren through no choice of her own. If only they could make it through the next seven days without fighting or falling out, Reem thought.

*

'It must be the sun,' Anthony joked in Reem's ear as he slipped his arm around her waist. 'That's it, I'm telling you. It's only the northern weather that turns your mother into a vampire. All she needed was the sun.' Reem elbowed him to stop it, laughing herself. But the first three days of their holiday had passed without incident. Reem could hardly believe it.

Their square, whitewashed villa was in a small hillside town to the east of Nice overlooking Cap Ferrat. The villa was filled with light. There were sparkling sea views from almost every single room, the ocean as still and as thick blue as a child's poster paint. Upstairs each bedroom had its own balcony, draped with cascades of shocking pink bougainvillea as bright as nail polish. The sun continued to burn high in the sky each day but the children, overjoyed by the luxury of a large garden and a private pool, did not complain of discomfort like they did back home in Brighton where the sea air felt heavy in the summer and smelt like fatty food. Here the sweet fragrance of flowers lingered and followed in their shadows, touching their tanned shoulders like blessings.

With the children constantly seeking her attention, Reem's mother was happy. On the second day, she had gone for a walk early in the morning and happened to notice a small bakery a few minutes away. She returned quickly, slightly out of breath, to ask if she could take the children there before the pavements turned too hot, and then the three of them returned with fresh, flaky croissants for everyone to share. Her mother had done this the next morning too, taking Sami by the hand and strapping Lila into her stroller while Reem and Anthony lay in bed in each other's arms. 'See,' Anthony said, kissing her hair and nibbling her neck. 'I told you it would work out just fine.'

They drove to the town and her mother walked ahead with Sami and Lila, pointing at the yachts in the harbour, while Reem and Anthony walked hand in hand a little way behind. At the white sandy beach, her mother rolled up her trousers above her ankles and stood looking out at the glittering sea, her face soft in the creases. More than once, Reem had wanted to ask her what she was thinking about, but she never did, because they had never talked that way. Reem thought her mother seemed happier than she had seen her in a long time, though this made her feel guiltier still, as if she should have asked her mother to come on holiday with them long ago. 'If this goes well,' Reem said to Anthony, undressing at the end of the day out of the full-length dress she'd chosen to wear with a tee-shirt underneath the straps, 'I'll ask her to come to Brighton and stay for a few days. For the kids.'

Most nights after the children had gone to bed, her mother insisted Anthony and Reem go out alone, saying she would fix herself a lighter meal from the food in the fridge. They did not resist and so Reem and Anthony ate out, just the two of them, at cosy seafood restaurants in the harbour, holding hands between forkfuls under the glow of festoon lights and flickering candles. It had been months since they had done this.

It required some effort, though, to keep the shell of peace. Reem made sure to dress carefully so as to avoid any unnecessary criticisms, wearing long skirts and dresses with loose airy tops layered underneath to cover her upper arms, or the skin below her collarbone, even though she had still packed her shorts and yearned to feel the golden sun warm upon her skin. Every now and again came small judgements dressed up as concern: a remark on the children's behaviour as a reflection on Reem's poor mothering, an observation on Anthony's careless way with money as a sign of his unreliability, a caution that Lila should not stay out too long in the sun for fear her skin would turn too dark. Occasionally there were questions that may have seemed perfectly innocent but which knowingly pricked away at Reem's insecurities; had she lost all her pregnancy weight yet, had she considered laser hair removal for the facial hair she threaded, just in case it got thicker, because did she know it could with age? It took effort for Reem to let these little things go, reminding herself that this was just the way things were between them, and besides, Anthony and the children lightened the mood. Mostly she managed to let the words dissipate into the air and drift away like the petals that fell from the bougainvillea whenever the children brushed past.

On the fourth day, over a picnic lunch of baguettes and cheese salad, Reem's mother began telling Anthony about a relative he hadn't yet met, a cousin of Reem's who had recently moved from Lahore to Manchester. 'She's a lovely girl,' she said. 'She always phones, asks if I want to come over on the weekend. She understands that in our culture, we look after our elders, you know? She takes such good care of me, I'm so glad for her company.' Then she turned to Reem and said, 'You should invite her to Brighton, I will give you her number,' and Reem said nothing but nodded, knowing that what her mother was really trying to say, trying to show, was that her cousin did more for her mother than she ever did.

Later that day, Reem waited until her mother had gone up to her room for a nap to swim in the pool with the children, something she had been desperate to do as the heat blazed unbearable at times, but which she knew she could not with her mother around. When she tiptoed out onto the terrace, her legs and arms and stomach bare in a black bikini, Anthony wolf-whistled and yelled, 'Mama's breaking all the rules!' and Reem, smiling, told him to keep it down.

*

On the fifth day, they took a day trip to a lavender farm an hour's drive away. The air was dry and the dusky scent surrounded them like a haze. Reem found it enchanting but the children grew afraid of the chubby bumblebees bumping into their knees. Anthony took them to the café for ice cream, leaving Reem alone with her mother in the vastness of the flower field. They walked slowly, Reem leading and her mother following behind, treading their way lightly through the endless rows of wild bushes, which glowed under the sun like clusters of gemstones, catching the light on their angled tips. Reem trailed her hand atop the flower buds, every now and again bringing her palm up to her nose to inhale the deep perfume stained on her fingers.

'Are you having a nice time, Ma?' Reem asked.

'I am,' her mother replied politely. 'Thank you so much for having me.' They walked on in silence.

'It was nice of you to ask me to join you,' she added slowly. 'I know you are very busy these days with Sami and Lila but sometimes I do feel like you have forgotten me.'

'I haven't forgotten you, Ma, it's just, you know.'

'I know, I was a mother too. I still am. And one day you too will know what it feels like to miss your child. What would you do if Lila or Sami stopped phoning you, if you only saw them twice a year?'

Reem let out a little puff of air, still walking ahead, aware of what turn the conversation was taking and regretting having started it.

'Brighton is so far away, Ma,' she said, defensively. 'It's not my fault the train takes so long.'

'I never said it was your fault,' her mother said. 'But it does not take much to pick up the phone. I feel lonely but now I have your cousin. Look what she does. She is so good, honestly. She has invited me to her home for a week when I return.'

Reem shook her head impatiently. 'Here we go,' she muttered and then louder and flatter, 'You've made your point. I'm going back to the car.'

'There, I can't say anything to her. She can never listen,' her mother said. 'Always, she is the same,' she said, as if she were talking to the angry bees. 'Stupid girl, stupid, selfish girl!' Her mother's voice was like a slammed door. Reem turned around fast like a whirlwind to face her but though she had so many things she wanted to say, like how she was trying so hard, like how nothing she ever did was good enough anyway, when she opened her mouth nothing came. She only shook her head, shrugged her shoulders helplessly and turned away again, the gap between them widening as Reem walked faster and her mother tried to keep up. On the drive home, Reem studied a pamphlet she had picked up from the farm while pretending nothing was wrong. 'Lavender represents not only good luck and devotion but it can also mean distrust,' she read. She crumpled it up, let it fall under her seat.

*

The next morning Reem pulled out her denim shorts, which cut so high on her thighs they were hot pants really, and a strappy vest, and put them on over her black bikini. She had thrown these into her suitcase last minute, although she hadn't planned on wearing them. It was only the morning but already nearly forty degrees and she felt the air conditioning pressing into her hard, curling like a fist. She knew she was behaving like a child, could see the petulance in her own face as she looked in the mirror, but she had also had enough. They were leaving tomorrow anyway.

Anthony, who was already downstairs making coffee, raised his eyebrows at her as she came down the stairs into the open plan kitchen and lounge. Her mother sat at the dining table in front of the sliding patio doors that led to the terrace. She was talking to the children, teaching them the word for milk in Urdu, when she saw Reem stride towards them. At first, her expression was blank as if she did not realise that it was Reem but some other woman, tall, proud and scantily dressed. Then her face seemed to fold, turning darkly.

Reem kissed the tops of her children's heads, one by one, and pulled out a chair to sit down with them, opposite her mother. 'Hey, little ones,' she said. 'What are you all up to over here?' She looked straight ahead at her mother. At first her mother said nothing. Then, after a while she asked, 'What is all this for?'

'All what?'

'This scene, this – these things you are wearing.'

'Oh, I've had them for years.'

Her mother nodded slowly. 'I see. So this is all because I said one thing to you yesterday? I can't even express my opinion, is that it?'

'I've had enough of listening to your opinion. I've had to hear it my whole life,' Reem spat, spitefulness rolling around her tongue.

Her mother pushed her chair back. 'I see,' she said again and she began saying things in Urdu in a low voice, muttering so Reem could not hear.

'Speak English,' Reem said. 'Speak English,' she shouted as her mother left the room and went up the stairs.

Anthony came forward to stop her, to tell her that was enough, but Reem pushed past him and followed her mother upstairs. He called her name and tried to catch her by the wrist but she flinched and shot him a warning look and so he backed away, an expression of dread on his face.

Upstairs, Reem flung open her mother's door. Her mother, small and crouched, sat on the bed with her head in her hands.

'You always do this,' Reem's voice was dark and throaty. 'What the fuck does it matter what I wear? I'm an adult. Nothing I do is ever good enough for you anyway, you really think I care what you think? You think I care? You always do this, you ruin everything!' Reem kept going, her words pummelling like stones. Her mother just kept shaking her head and then she stood and moved to the balcony door, bruised shafts of violet morning light breaking on the deep blue sea sparkling in the distance behind her. Her mother's voice frayed at the edges as she turned to face Reem and said, 'I sometimes think, what did I do? To be punished with a daughter like you. Ever since you were a girl, you have been nothing but trouble for me. Look at you. I thank God your father never had to hear the way you talk to me, see the woman you have become.'

It took only a moment for Reem to step forward, her hands moving wildly as she kept yelling, her voice gravelly, and only another moment still for her mother to retreat with her hands in the air as though she were a thief caught mid-steal, backing away through the balcony door, towards the rusty balustrade. Reem reached out, her hand firm on her mother's shoulder. Her mother was saying something with a panic in her eyes, but Reem could not hear exactly what for the blood rushed about like ribbons of loose wind tangling through her head, but then, just like that, her mother lost her balance and stumbled backwards again. She reached behind herself for the rail and shifted her weight, only all of a sudden the balustrade gave way and as it did, she fell, right over the balcony's edge. Reem jumped to the side and though she opened her mouth, nothing came; she would never forget the pink petals of the bougainvillea scattering like sad little paper hearts falling in slow motion, nor the headiness of the flowers' cloying perfume, nor her mother's spotless white trainers tumbling through the hot air, thick like honey.

# Firecracker

It's the night before my wedding and you lie barefoot on my hotel bed lounging back on the pillows as if you own the place. Remote control in one hand, your shoes strewn across the floor, your crumpled clothes discarded in a trailing heap. I shake them out, fold them up, place them in a neat pile on the sideboard.

*You could at least…!* I say and you laugh, make some joke about how you hope my forthcoming marriage to the boyfriend you never particularly liked might lighten up my austere, tidy ways. I maybe laugh too but honestly I am not joking for I have always hated this habit of yours, the messy carelessness that means I am forever picking up after you while you are forever losing things. Pieces of jewellery, library books, your mobile phone.

Eventually this will happen to us. You will drop bits of our friendship here and there and eventually, I will stop picking us back up, picking you back up, putting us back together again. Eventually we might forget where we put it, this friendship of ours, and we will both let it fall through the cracks of a floorboard, forgotten in the memory of old mix tapes and letters boxed in an attic somewhere.

But tonight you fall asleep on my bed. I nudge you with my foot, shake your shoulder. We have shared many milestones but I want to be on my own tonight. *Alright, alright!* and you smile your fabulous crooked smile and slope out of my room into yours next door. The next morning, you are late to my wedding. I don't even know when you arrive. Later I will wonder if this was the moment things changed. The moment you practically missed my wedding because you were drunk, passed out in your room. The moment I kicked you out of my room into your own. The moment you started losing me, we started losing each other. But then I realise: it had already happened long, long before.

*

We meet at university. We are eighteen. The way you tell the story, you say you stood in my doorway and talked and talked and talked so much that I begrudgingly invited you into my room just to shut you up. You tell people we stayed up talking so late, you fell asleep on my floor. This part is untrue but I stopped correcting you a long time ago.

Truth is, you always stay too long. *I am literally throwing you out right now!* I yell and you cackle and duck as I throw your scarf or your jumper at your head. In this way you are like the sibling I have never had; annoying, but beloved in equal measure.

At university I routinely pick up all the things you scatter in my room over the course of an average day – a cardigan, a hairband, eyeliner, lip balm, a bunch of old magazines – and place them outside your door when you are asleep. Sometimes you mess up my bookshelves or my desk on purpose. *Would you look at that*, you say. *Oops.*

Despite your attitude to orderliness, I am drawn to you by the way you talk endlessly and the things you say and this is how we become friends in the first place. You talk like poetry. You fizz like lemonade, bittersweet; you do not care what other people think of your clothes or the wild way you dance. You are dreamlike, with the sort of face that does not even need make-up. Many boys fall in love with you and later so too will many men but you pretend not to care. One night you decide to kiss as many boys as you can; it is a game to you. You are writing a book already and you have this air of knowing artfulness and because I trust you, I show you the short stories I have written that I have never shown anyone else (even though you never show me anything you have written yourself).

It does not take me long to understand that your stream of talking is some kind of front because there are other edges to you, frail edges. Sometimes you cloud over. You disappear. You fade out as though I've lost you for a minute or two to some other frequency, some other conversation in your head. *Hey*, I say, *Where'd you go?* And you blink, shake your head and smile and that's always the end of it.

You let things slip about your parents, how you feel like an awkward piece of inherited furniture they are obliged to hold onto. You were in trouble at school and because of this your father gives up on you and calls you chaotic, misspent. You tell me you feel rootless and times like these, when your sad thoughts empty out like lonely pennies, I squeeze your hand because I know you do not share this with anyone else but then you disappear, a will-o'-the-wisp, into that other place in your head again.

You are witty, clever, but you skip lectures all the time and you are not the least bit concerned. All you read are back copies of *Vogue*. You say you don't care about studying because of the book you are writing, which someone in publishing had told you showed great promise. The entirety of university is like a gap year to you, an escape from your parents to do whatever you want to do and boy, you do everything you can get your hands on. But me, I fret a lot over my grades, over my future, about being sensible and making the right choices. Times like these you pull me up onto my feet to dance. *You take things too seriously*, you tell me, head thrown back, drink in hand. *But Lou*, I want to say. *You don't take things seriously enough*.

You stay with me over the long summer holidays. Because you talk so damn much you charm my parents with your chattiness and your beauty, your livewire energy. *Firecracker*, my mother calls you. One night you tell me you love my life and I burst out laughing because

I know you cannot mean it because I am ordinary and grew up in the suburbs but you grew up in London and everything about you is bespoke. *But I do*, you say. *I mean it entirely.*

*

We graduate. I try not to make a big deal of it because you did not do as well as the rest of us and even though you say you do not care, I know you do.

The rest of us are making plans for our futures. I line up unpaid internships on magazines because eventually I want to be the sort of writer who might even get paid and because we both want to write for a living I offer to share the contacts I make. But you tell me you have other plans, plans for the book you've been writing ever since before we started university. Your cheeks burn, your skin glows, and you say you still can't tell me more about it yet, but that it's going to happen for you, your book, your name in print. I believe you, I tell you, *I believe in you*, even though you've never shown me a word you've written.

You insist I stay with you in your parents' flat in west London while I'm interning and you squeal like a small child at the prospect of us playing house. Your parents are away and so at first my stay feels hilarious, a carefree holiday, but my days interning are long and uninspiring. In the frustration of working for free, I spend my evenings searching online for paid work.

I stay up late applying for junior roles on newspapers, writing cover letters, drafting emails to editors. You leave me be initially (besides, you tell me you are writing your book) but soon you begin to constantly interrupt. *Come out for ice cream! Let's get pizza!* you say. Or *Dance! I want to dance!* You do not knock, you never knock, and when you say these things it is always late at night when I am in my pyjamas and you are in some wacky outfit, your eyes burning bright as though you are on fire. *I am trying to find work,* I say. *Lou, I have stuff to do.* Times like this you make me mad. In my head, I want to say, *What's wrong with you? How old are you, like five?* But finally you give up. You shut my door without a wisecrack and you leave without messing anything up.

We begin to see less of each other even though we live in the same place. Sometimes you are gone for days. There are times I don't hear from you and then when I do, your messages make little sense, odd manic messages that I think are made-up but I cannot be sure. *I am in Paris! Looking for a cat! I have gone to Camden to buy a hat! I am working on my prologue from a man's bed!*

You lose your keys at least three times a week. Sometimes you blow hot and cold like a monsoon storm. I overhear you arguing with your parents on the phone and though your face is shadowed and stained afterwards and though I try to tell you I'm here for you, you pretend like it never happened at all. One night I find you curled up, bruised and crying on the floor and yet still you do not tell me what's wrong.

At university you were always what our other friends called *Random* because you did things like quote Shakespeare to strangers and wear daisy garlands and summer dresses in the thick of winter and because you also did that thing whereby you went somewhere else in your head, but I always stood up for you. *She's not strange*, I would say. *She's poetic. Creative. Give her a break.*

I always loved your ability to see wit and beauty in ordinary things. But now your intensity is making my head spin because I do not know what's going on with you, because you will not tell me what it means when you slam the window or the door or lock yourself in the bathroom. You do not like meeting up with our other friends any more and I make excuses for you in front of them. They ask how you are only now I do not know what to say so I sigh, *Hard times*. They ask if you have a job and I shake my head. *To be honest I never really understood how come the two of you were such good friends,* one of them says.

Meanwhile your flat is a mess. It is more than a mess. It is dirty. I come back from interning and open the windows, make your bed. At university this too was part of your charm; your unbrushed hair, the romance of an abundance of vintage clothes draped on the back of a chair. But here in the real world, it is petulant, lazy. *Laissez-faire*, you say as I vacuum around you. Washing your dishes, doing your laundry. I am grateful for having a place to stay but I am angry with you for living this way.

I ask how your book is going. You tell me it's nearly finished.

I get a job on a newspaper with a decent enough salary and because I have met someone and because I need normality and space and somewhere clean to live, I want to rent a flat of my own. But I feel guilty for even thinking it, more guilty than you will ever know, as though I am leaving you behind. But I am beginning to hate living with you. It is too much, like overwhelming perfume that turns my stomach, hurts my head. I have to move.

Years later I will see a film about a young woman in north London who died in her flat and wasn't found for three years and for weeks I will have nightmares that the young woman could have been you.

*

When your parents return I leave, even though I hate myself for doing this to you. I do not know if you ever forgive me for leaving you with them but you watch me pack with a rage burning on your skin. *Be seeing you, hope not sporadically*, you flatly say, a line from some dumb movie we both liked, as you shut the door.

But without the pressure of living alone just the two of us, the fever of our strange friendship breaks like the relief of rain in high summer. There is a space between us now and at first the space is empty but then it widens into a space in which we are eventually able to come together again.

I write you a letter. I tell you it all felt too much but I also tell you that I miss you, that I trust you, that I care and worry about you because you have distanced yourself from so many of our friends and I do not want you to distance yourself from me. When you receive it, you call me and even though I am at work, I pick up straight away because I hoped you would call, because I knew you would. You open with a burst of laughter that sounds like a rainbow and then: *Look at us! We're like an old married couple!* You laugh some more and so I do too and then you sniff and say, *Sorry for being A Nightmare.* You say you've been thinking it over and the problem is we don't do stuff together any more and so that's what we begin to do, *stuff*; dancing, movies, cocktails and though it takes a few months to find our rhythm for a while it is as though we are back at university again.

I have my own place now and when you first come to visit you run your finger along the mantlepiece and say *Hmm* like Mary Poppins, which cracks us both up. You often come over and still stay too late. You have lost weight so I feed you carbs, baked potatoes as big as our heads, and you talk and talk and talk and we laugh and laugh and laugh and though I always plan to talk to you about it properly, face-to-face, about those months when I stayed with you and you seemed like you were falling apart, weekends like these reassure me that you are okay, that you are not lost, that you are not lonely or being left behind.

One time when you're raiding my fridge, you tell me how you feel so frozen some days you physically cannot move. You're seeing a therapist now and finding your way through the dark and you just throw this information out there and then you tell me I'm out of milk. You switch the subject back to the boy I'm dating and you tease me about him like a teen, asking ridiculous questions about his kissing technique. I throw a cushion at your head and you stick your tongue out at me on your way to the fold-out sofa bed.

After you leave, I always find something you have left behind. A crumpled train ticket. A bottle of perfume. A hairbrush. It is as though you do it on purpose.

*

We turn thirty. I have just got engaged.

*Do you really love him?* you want to know and the way you say it, it's with a hint of distaste. I say I do and then you press me for more, but I keep it to myself because you sleep with men but you do not fall in love with them and I do not want to make you feel judged or alone. You joke about me being married and having babies and moving to the suburbs and I let you make that joke before asking if you'll ever settle down, have a proper relationship now. You almost spit your coffee out with laughter and then you call yourself a spinster, somebody's mistress at best, but there's a sadness behind the way you say it so then I don't ever bring the subject up again.

The first time you meet him, the man who will eventually ask me to be his wife, you turn up in a polka dot dress with a stiff petticoat underneath it, like fancy dress, and you talk lickety-split, a character from a cartoon. Later I ask him what he thinks of you. He smiles and says you're a little crazy, like a whirlwind, which is something people have often said about you. *Wouldn't put the two of you together is all*, he calls from the kitchen. I smile too, because I imagine you must think the same about him and me.

Yet several months later you throw yourself into my wedding with a fervour that surprises me especially because I do not even ask it of you. I don't even want a hen-do but you press one upon me with such unprecedented enthusiasm, giddy and girly, I don't stop you. You gather the friends I love together like flowers, even the ones who used to be your friends too, the ones with whom you had fallen out of touch. When you are with them you act as though you had never deliberately distanced yourself from them at all. You decorate the restaurant with fairy lights and gauzy drapes and it's all so theatrical, all so pretty, and I'm all so touched, I cry.

*I just want to do this for you*, you whisper in my ear. I feel bad for saying it but honestly, I didn't think you could pull it off.

But despite all this, a couple of weekends later you still pass out drunk in your hotel room the night before my wedding and end up missing most of it and that's when I really begin to wonder what the hell is wrong with you.

*

After my honeymoon, you turn up on my doorstep with flowers and a basket of biscuits, a tulle ribbon in your hair. It's only flowers and only biscuits and you missed my wedding for God's sake, but I still forgive you. I forgive you because I feel sorry for you. But I also forgive you because I care. You tell me you don't know why you acted the way you did, that things got out of hand, that you drank because you were a little sad and felt frozen again. *The ice is melting now*, you say.

I forgive you because I wish things had turned out differently for you. I wish you had parents who prioritised you and I wish you felt loved and I wish something had become of the book you told us all you were writing because honestly, I think that might have saved you most of all. I forgive you because you're still that person who charmed me utterly into being her friend, stood in my doorway, talking and talking and talking of marvellous, unbelievable things.

But then you go dark. Of all the things to do, you disappear, you go dark. You turn your landline off and your mobile phone off too and I cannot reach you at all. I think about that film I had seen with the young woman with lots of friends but also no friends, lying dead and undiscovered for years and now, now that so much has passed, I begin to believe that might actually, truly, happen to you too.

Then out of the blue weeks and weeks later you come back, as though nothing has happened at all. I'm mad at you but you tease me, call me *Worrywart* in a sing-song voice. You tell me you're researching your book and I know that this is a total lie because every time in the last twelve years that I have asked you about it, you are never able to give anything away.

You turn your phone on, you turn it off. I can't keep track of where you're at.

*

I have a baby. I think of you from time to time.

I invite you round for lunch because I haven't seen you for over seven months when I told you I was pregnant and I haven't heard from you since my baby was born, apart from a text message of *Congrats!* when I sent you a photo the day after he arrived. *Are you sure you want her to come?* my husband asks and I say yes, because I get the feeling that if I don't call you over, I might not ever see you again.

We all have those friends, the ones we can go months without seeing yet it feels like no time at all has passed when they walk in the door. We all have those friends who ground us. But you are not that sort of friend and this feeling of ease, of comfort and long-term connection does not come into my home with you.

It is a strange lunch, strange in its mundanity. You have a job now, an assistant in some tech start-up, and from this I deduce your book never did come out, if it was even written at all. You talk so politely, it is as though you are holding it in, the sharp smartass comments about my decline into domesticity, a baby attached to my breast, a tidy three-bedroom house. You hold my baby and he tugs your necklace off and then you pass him back to me.

I wish I could say there had been some drama, that we had some falling out when we sat down to the table for our lasagne lunch, if only to make sense of how our friendship went from being so all-consuming to merely a memory of my twenties. If only to understand how you went from being someone who always stayed too long, someone I had to literally shove out the door, to being someone I just happened to know some time ago.

I text you to thank you for coming but you never reply. I wonder if perhaps you've lost your phone so later at Christmas I send you a card and then another on your birthday too. In between I email, nothing much, simply wondering how you are, but you never write back so I stop then. But I am not angry at you. I understand. I accept time has passed and we have changed and there is an emptiness now in which we have nothing left to say because it has all been said already, because there are no words left between us any more.

When you come over that last time, you leave a necklace behind, still as forgetful as you ever were. It has an initial on it, only the initial is not even for your name. I do not know whose initial it is. It is another one of those inexplicable wildcard things about you. For a while I keep the necklace safe in a small envelope in the back of a drawer with the intention of giving it back to you when I see you again, but then one day when I am tidying up I set it aside to give to charity.

It is only later that I remember how it even came to be there.

# The Jam Maker

There had never been a summer like it.

That was what everyone in the village said when they stopped by our cottage and sat with my mother around our kitchen table, offering their quiet condolences alongside small, neighbourly offerings of one-pot dinners, bottles of milk, loaves of bread. Even I remembered the previous year, the sad soggy rain that lasted all summer long and made my mother cry and turn to my father in despair to say: Why of all places did you have to come here? But this new summer, this particular summer, was as perfectly formed as a china tea set; an endless run of exquisite clear blue skies and bright sun cooled by a string of steady breezes. In the afternoons, lazy white clouds rolled through the sky like long cats, casting a thin shade before dissolving to let the sun stretch into the evenings again. It would have been the perfect summer, if not for my father's death.

*

The afternoon of the day my father died, he took me strawberry picking up at Cross Meadows. It was a Sunday, the only day his surgery was closed. My father and I spent Sundays together because my mother, always complaining what a dust trap the dark beams across the low ceilings were, liked to stay home and clean the cottage. She would shoo us out the door like chickens so she could wash the windows and sweep away the cobwebs that stretched wraithishly across the corners of the walls, and this meant my father and I were free to do whatever we wanted to for hours. Some Sundays we would roam the woods or walk down to the mere and along the way he would teach me how to identify the ash trees from the oaks, point out which of the wild, rambling brambles we could pick and eat and which were best left alone. Other times, we would drive an hour to Birmingham for fish and chips, or watch a film if it was raining. But that particular Sunday in the middle of July in 1985, hours before he died, we went strawberry picking.

Pick the brightest ones! my father said with a wink as he popped several in his mouth all at once and I did the same, tasting the grit of mud mixed with the smart of a fresh strawberry, my small knees dusty from crouching in dry earth to seek out the best, plumpest ones. I grew tired and my father hoisted me up onto his shoulders, and I felt something then that I later came to know was contentment. Later, when I confided in my mother about my memories of this part of the day, the golden hours before my father died, she sort of scoffed and said: You worshipped him, so you only remember the good bits. After that, I stopped telling her what I remembered any more.

*

When we came home that afternoon with three bursting punnets of strawberries, my mother looked the pair of us up and down, her stare lingering at my earth-stained knees, and said: But why so many? My father held up the overstuffed cardboard baskets like trophies in response and said triumphantly: One for each of us! But my mother shook her head and said: They will go bad, they will not last, they never do.

My father and I were eating strawberries in the garden for lunch, my mother preferring to warm a small bowl of lentils for herself instead, when the phone rang and, sure enough, it was a patient with a summer cold requesting that my father make a house call. My father never complained about interruptions from his patients, although my mother always did, muttering about how much of his time they took up, saying things like: All day at the surgery, then even when you come home; every little thing these people call you for. She never spoke in English though, the way my father did. It was always in her own language.

My father came back into the garden, wiped the corners of his mouth on a napkin, kissed the top of my head and announced he was leaving. He stopped to kiss my mother on the cheek, though she did not look at him, and then he left. My mother said: Now what? She sighed at our mountain of ruby-hued pickings and spent the rest of the afternoon in the kitchen, hulling and chopping and simmering strawberries in sugar, muttering crossly again and again in her language that she had a hundred and one better things to do. I stood in the doorway, sad to see she was chopping all of them, that soon there would be no fresh strawberries left. I lingered, unsure whether to offer to help, for often she would snap at me even if my intentions were good. But then she caught me watching her and her serious face softened and she said: Come!

So I ran to her side and, for a moment, as we stirred and thickened the bubbling strawberries, I felt as though I was standing inside a children's book, this sort of softness from my mother being a rare kind of magic. She plunged her hand into one of the remaining punnets and said: See, already they are too soft, already they are spoiled. The way she said it, I was not sure if she was sad about it or if it was my fault, for having picked them in the first place. She kept chopping, I kept stirring. Every now and then she nodded in the direction of the pan and said sharply in her language, Be careful, watch it doesn't burn or offered other such instructions. The liquid in the pan began to thicken into something more congealed, dark red and viscous, and the bubbles began to roll to the surface slower then, as though they were trapped underneath. See, she said, almost there. I watched my mother tip the sugar in, spoon by spoon, like little clouds of vanishing dust, neither of us saying a word.

On the way home that day from his house call, my father's car collided with two others and a hedgerow.

For days the cottage smelt lovely, like spun sugar, even though my father's heart had stopped.

*

Though he was in many ways an outsider, my father was well-liked and well-known in the village. As the local doctor, it seemed everyone was his patient and wherever we went together, people stopped to say hello and shake his hand. He made friends with neighbours up and down the lane, exchanging shoots from fruit trees over garden gates and inviting some of them over for tea, which put my mother out greatly. On the main street he stopped to talk to every shop owner, every fellow customer, asking after their families and their numerous ailments. I still have proof of this, of how well-liked he was, from the condolence cards I collected and kept in a biscuit tin, even though my mother always said cards were pointless and such an *English* thing.

*

Once my father bought my mother a miniskirt from one of the large department stores in Birmingham, more than an hour's drive away. At home he coaxed her to try it on, and though she blushed and turned this way and that in the hallway mirror with her hands on her hips, and though my father and I clapped our hands and told her she looked beautiful, she quickly changed back into her tunic and trousers and said to my father and me not to be so silly.

Sometimes after she had collected me from school, my mother walked me to my father's surgery and left me there to do my homework while she returned home, to be alone. I would sit with my school books open in the reception, a dark, shady room that smelt of mulberries and rain, while waiting for my father to finish for the day. On one of those afternoons, I noticed Miss Pattie, my father's receptionist, wearing the exact same skirt he had picked out for my mother, thinking what a coincidence that was. On these afternoons, Miss Pattie fed me chocolate biscuits and put the radio on, singing and dancing behind the reception desk if there were no more patients waiting, while I marvelled at the way that she moved.

Some evenings after dinner my father walked down to meet friends from the cricket club at The Heart and Arrows, cricket being in our blood he said, although my mother did not approve of this one bit. The first time he went, she was so upset she locked the door and put the latch on. He pleaded with her to let him back in, which she only did after he had begun to recite couplets from her favourite poet Faiz Ali Faiz quite loudly. She rushed him in, asking in their language if he had gone crazy, telling him to be quiet, for what would the neighbours think?

Some Sundays, my father begged my mother to leave the cleaning and come with us on our walks to the woods or down to the mere or out for lunch, but my mother always said no and in this way, the times he asked her grew fewer and further in between. Once, just as we were about to leave for the cinema in Birmingham, my father whispered to me: What if we ask Miss Pattie to come along? I adored Miss Pattie because she painted her nails berry-red and had fair hair like a doll and a shiny smile like one too, so I said: Yes! I climbed into the backseat as we pulled up outside her tiny two-up two-down and she bounced into the car, filling it with the scent of spring, all daisies and buttercups. At the cinema she sat between my father and me, and every now and again, she leaned over and touched my hair. Later, after we had dropped Miss Pattie outside her house and she had turned to blow a kiss and winked and waved, my father turned to me and put his fingers to his lip and said: Let's not tell Amma, okay?

Whenever my father and I returned to the cottage on Sundays, my mother's mood was always a shade darker. After scrubbing the cottage clean, she sat cross-legged in the middle of the double bed she shared with my father and made trunk calls to her sisters. Once, I overheard her speaking to them, aunts I had not yet met, in her language on the phone. Though my understanding of my mother's language was never particularly good, I think what she had said was: My heart, it is hurting here.

*

One afternoon some weeks after my father's death, my mother announced we were moving to a town on the other side of the city. I had been to this town before. Every three months my father drove my mother there to stock up on spices, bagged meat, shawls and cassettes of films with titles I did not understand, all the things she missed. We went into shop after shop, one after the other, each smelling like the inside of a suitcase. My mother's favourite store was a fabric emporium. She spent hours in here, pulling out roll after roll of bright-coloured cottons and silks, discussing patterns of tunics she might stitch while I sat on the floor with a fizzy drink the shop owner had handed me and my father smoked cigarettes outside or waited in the car.

My mother was a different mother in this town. Sometimes she went days without talking in the cottage, replying to my father's attempts to make conversation only with odd grunts or hard stares depending on her and his mood. Some days, she did not even talk to me. But in this town, she came alive. Her cheeks flushed and her eyes shone with excitement and when she spoke it was like a song. She bought me treats, bright orange spirals of fried sugar that made the tips of my fingers sticky, and I sucked on these and watched her, wondering which version of my mother was real; this one, or the one who lived with us in the cottage. I think that what she hoped for more than anything on these day trips to this town was that someone might have befriended us and invited us to their house for tea, but we were not from here. Every time we visited, she asked my father to drive up and down past rows of terraced houses, trying to convince him to move while my father scorned the lack of space, the way the houses were so boxed in, the way everyone looked the same. Why, he said to her, would you want to live here, when you cannot even flush the toilet without a neighbour hearing? One time my parents argued because my mother had wanted to stay longer and my father had said: But I have left all of this behind. They spoke in their language, too fast and too angry for me to fully understand, but I think what my mother said in reply was: You are so ashamed, are you not?

I did not want to move to this town, which some English people and even my father called Little India in a not very kind way. I liked where we lived. I liked it very much. I liked our quiet village and its tidy row of stores on the main street and its stone cottages and the mere and the green and the cricket club. Though I was a lonely, bookish sort of girl and did not particularly have any friends, I still liked school. I liked the library and the tuck shop and wearing a ribbon around my straw hat, pulling my white socks up to my knees. It seemed to me the more I did these things, the more I might become like the characters in the books I read, the ones with cheery mothers who wore neckerchiefs and gingham skirts and prepared picnic baskets all ready-set-go for adventures, though I knew my mother was never going to be like one of those mothers at all. Since my father's sudden death, my mother was so preoccupied with paperwork and phone calls, frowning over the desk in the nook my father called his study, that I spent more and more time alone during these summer holidays. I spent hours each day walking mindlessly down to the mossy mere or sitting on the edge of the cricket pitch instead, a book unopened on my lap. Once, I found myself quite unexpectedly knocking on Miss Pattie's door, hoping she might invite me in and feed me treats and let me watch television with her on her couch with her arm around me, but she only peeped at me from behind the front door with pink-rimmed eyes and said quietly: Go home love, you should not be here.

Often I roamed the woods, returning home only when I grew hungry. Sometimes I ran wildly, not caring about the nettles fingering my shins. Other times I sat still under the shade of a tree, watching, listening, and at these times, I felt my father around me; in the blades of grass, in the papery wings of the butterflies that brushed my bare legs and the rough bark of the trees. I did not want to leave this place.

But that afternoon, my mother spoke in her language in a thick low voice and said: We should be with people who are like us. Outside, a canopy of thin clouds rolled over the sky and pale shadows passed along the wall. I could only twitch my fingers. My mother was severe and I suppose this made me a passive child, not prone to crying out loud nor banging my fists in anger, and I was rarely ever disobedient, but just then I felt something splinter. I ran out of the kitchen door and through the front gate, sobbing in heaps for the first time since my father had died. I heard my mother call after me but I ran far away from her into the woods until finally I could run no more and I threw myself down onto the ground, breathless and panting.

I lay there for a long time, my face pressed sideways into the dry earth. Down here, deep in the woods secluded from the sun, a faint chill laced through the sycamore trees, prickling my bare arms. From where I was lying I could see shoots of summer grass, sheaths of wild sweet ferns laden with sap nodding in my direction, clusters of bright buttercups shining like splashes of sunshine. White butterflies flapped like scraps of paper tossed in the air. The earth pulsed. In the distance I saw clumps of blackberry bushes, bubbling and ripe, and a thick growth of gooseberries, and then I noticed the scrappy edges of the magenta stems my father had taught me to strictly avoid because of their poison. I scrambled to my knees and picked my way through towards the crowded hedgerows until I reached the dark, shiny berries sticking out of their strange stems, red for danger. I fingered the hostile shape of their glossy lance-like leaves for a moment and then, without thinking, I snapped the stems and gathered as much of the fruit my father had warned me not to touch as I could, filling my pockets, staining my hands.

\*

Back home, I set to work immediately, my mother still busy in my father's nook, making calls to enquire after rooms to rent in Little India. I chopped the berries as quickly as I could and tumbled them into a heavy pan. I held my breath as I lit the stove, something I was never normally allowed to do. I stirred as the berries thickened and turned foamy over the heat of the flames, fascinated to witness their transformation from shiny round pellets into a strange, sticky substance that seemed both dangerous and delicious. I added the sugar, first tipping in one spoon at a time as I recalled my mother had done and then, in my nervous excitement, all in one go, keen to hurry along the process. The air smelt so ripe, so thick and sweet, that it was hard to believe the berries were poisonous. I had made just enough to fill one large jar completely; I hoped it would be enough. I held the jar in my hands and turned it this way and that, inspecting the contents curiously. I observed how this jam was a more startling, potent shade of crimson than the strawberry one I had made with my mother the day my father died.

For the rest of the day, my mother remained behind my father's desk, sifting through bank statements and legal papers. When the jam had finally cooled to a thick sweet slurry, I approached her, shyly carrying the jam jar in one hand and a teaspoon in the other behind my back. In that moment, my mother looked older than she was, her hair scraped back hard, a hand upon her forehead, her shoulders hunched over. I lingered in the doorway, and then I stuck the jar out in front of me like a peace offering. I made jam, I said. She did not look up at me, still angry because I had run away from her even when she had called my name. I said: I made it for you, and only then did she look up at me.

She studied my face, as though contemplating how severely she ought to reprimand me for my earlier behaviour, and I held my breath, waiting. Then she tilted her head to the side, and her face softened for just a moment and she beckoned me towards her. Aao, come here, she said. Dikhao, show me.

I unscrewed the lid and she took the teaspoon from me. Somewhere beneath my dress, my small girl's heart beat hard between fear and anticipation. She dipped the spoon in like an arrow piercing a heart, the tip only just touching the potent jam. She licked it and then, quite unexpectedly, she stuck the spoon, scoop-side down, on her nose and crinkled it up. It was the first time I had ever seen her do such a thing and I laughed in astonishment at her absurdity. Then, as if she'd remembered herself, her mouth rearranged itself into a straight, thin line. She went back to her papers, while I waited and waited.

I was not sure how much jam I would need to give her for the poisonous berries to take hold, seep into her. Later that night, I crept out of my bed and over to hers, but she still stirred in her sleep and shifted on her pillow as my small shadow passed over her sleeping face. In the morning I watched as she reached for my jam and spread it thinly on her hard morning toast. She did this for three mornings and each time, my heart thumped. Still, nothing happened.

Our neighbours continued to leave baskets of food and groceries on our back step in the aftermath of my father's death, an act my mother considered more an inconvenience than a kindness, and loaves of bread and endless baked goods stacked up in the corner of the kitchen. Here, I found a batch of scones a neighbour had left for us and prepared one for her to have with her tea, the jam spread fatly in the middle, but she shook her head at me and left it untouched as she argued on the phone about the selling price of our cottage.

I was so exasperated that without even thinking about it, I walked over to Miss Pattie's house, carrying a plateful of the remaining scones layered with my poisonous jam in front of me. I thought I saw her curtain move but she did not come to the door and so I left them on her doorstep instead. I suspect she must have put the whole lot in the bin; they would have been stale, left out on a step uncovered on a warm day like that.

So in the end, because nothing had happened to anyone and because there was still three quarters of the contents of a large jam jar left, I ate the rest myself, straight out of the jar, all in one go, with a spoon. At first, I felt only stomach pains and then I fell into a fever that lasted two days, but that was it. A cry for attention, my mother said, crossly, refusing to even acknowledge that the poison was meant for her.

*

Little India was sandwiched between two major A roads and cordoned off by a motorway. There was no mere, there were no woods. In Little India, the air tasted like cumin and coriander and when the wind blew, I caught the smell of raw meat simmering in oil. Every day I looked up at the sky and I longed for the day that I might escape.

These days, I live in a village not dissimilar to the one in which I grew up, though I do not know if I belong here. It is a place where in the summer the fields over-spill with rapeseed and meadowsweet speckled like dots of sunlight and the night air is as thick as jelly, sticky with stars. They say this year's strawberries will be the plumpest crop yet.

*

There is a moment when you open a pot of home-made jam for the first time and the lid pops and you inhale the sweetness of soft, leathery fruit, when what you smell is not merely sugar and lemon and berries but a memory, a fragment, captured in time. This is what I tell my customers when they come into my little shop, enchanted by row upon row of glistening jam jars capturing each turn of the season in glass; childhood sweets and grandmas, velvet and violet, sunburn and rollerskates. But these are not my memories and now the scent of sugar-spun berries sickens me.

Decades have passed since I was that child who pre-served the crimson jelly of those poisonous berries. Now, when people come into my little shop – tour-ists who venture around these parts for the thatched cottages and the cream teas – charmed by the quintes-sential sweetness of my profession, they ask me how it is that I became a jam maker. They ask: Wherever did you learn such a lovely craft? When I tell them I learnt it from my Indian mother, for a moment their faces are frozen, in confusion, because there is nothing particu-larly romantic or quaintly English about that.

What I do not tell them is that every time I prepare a pot of thickening berries in my tiny kitchen behind the shopfront, hulling, chopping, boiling, stirring and add-ing just enough sugar so as to add a hint of something sweet but not so much as to make it sickly, I am reminded of dark things like loneliness and grief; other, emptier things I have not yet learnt to put a name to. People imagine my life is pretty. They exclaim: A jam maker! as though I must come from magic with fairy dust in my fingers, mixing potions of fig and rose, blackberry and bay. Lovers wrap up in my bed under crisp white sheets, mesmerised, for a woman who makes jam must surely be uncomplicated. Sometimes I wonder if I have chosen my line of work as some kind of punishment. This is what I think of as I stir and preserve, stir and preserve.

# Superstitious

When I was a teenager, I spent every summer with my girl-cousins in Lahore where there was little for us to do but wait until the day had cooled enough to venture out of their ceiling-fanned bedrooms and up onto the roof of my uncle's house, where we'd lie on charpoys and tell each other secrets, or lean over the roof railings and wolf whistle at boys riding by on motorbikes without their helmets on, and then crouch down and hide. My aunt was particular about propriety, as was (and still is) my mother, and so together they were always telling us off for laughing too loud or dancing or watching Bollywood films, but up on the roof we were free to giggle and gasp over the teen-girl magazines I'd secretly brought with me from England, full of articles on kissing techniques and double-page spreads of handsome boys. On the roof, we discarded our sandals and the dupattas we otherwise draped around our necks and we talked breathlessly about silly things like our future wedding days and the boys we thought we liked.

Once, as dusk fell and the sky turned pink, my girl-cousins pointed to the silhouette of a gnarly, silvery tree, on the periphery of their housing district. I understood that we were not supposed to go near it, my mother had mentioned it to me a few times, but I never did know why, until that night. My cousins told me that once there was a young woman who married for love, but her husband died in mysterious, unexplained circumstances. The story went that this young woman walked every night under the moonlight, searching for him, her love match, her heart broken. One night, her body was found, face-down and limbs twisted, at the foot of this tree. It was said that her hair had sewn itself into the tree's roots, each strand pinned into the dry earth, and it was said that her soul had been sucked into the hollow of its trunk, her grief weighing its boughs down forevermore. Apparently at night, you could hear her unborn baby cry.

The girls in the neighbourhood were forbidden from going anywhere near this tree, for fear the widow's spirit might taint them, infiltrate them somehow, and turn them into witches or, worse, future widows themselves. From that story came other superstitions, about djinns and the danger of wearing our hair loose or walking in the moonlight or doing both at the same time; the danger being that if we did, we might still lose our as-yet imaginary husbands. A love match, we exclaimed, at the wonder of it. A widow, we shuddered. How awful, we lamented, and then we threw our heads back and laughed and dared each other one by one.

Of course, I said I'd do it. And I did. I was the only one who made it all the way out to the tree and back, secretly slipping out of the gate while our parents took tea in the front room after dinner and our brothers played video games in the TV lounge. My girl-cousins whispered and watched from behind a window grille and promised they'd cover for me. I remember running as fast as I could, my heart beating wildly, my sandals rubbing my toes, the smell of jasmine heavy in the night air rushing past me. I remember the thrill of it and the fear of it; the very real possibility of being caught by my mother and my aunt but also my wilder terror of the widow and her spirit. Though I had told my girl-cousins that I thought the story silly, impossible and untrue, it frightened me. But still, I ran and I ran; terrified, exalted. I remember reaching out to touch the tree trunk, tagging it as though I was in a relay race, and my astonishment at how cold and smooth it felt, before I turned and ran straight back to the house, out of breath.

It's been years since I've spoken to my girl-cousins; we grew up, we lost touch, mostly because my brother and I stopped wanting to go to Lahore, convincing our parents to let us go on holiday to places like France and Italy like our school friends and their families instead. But now that I've become a sort of widow myself, I've found myself thinking of that night. I've found myself wondering if it's perhaps because of that night, because of that tree and my bravado and that silly, superstitious story, that this has happened to me. That this was always going to happen to me.

*

Some nights I find myself sitting in the shadow of the moon upon my floor before the windows, the dark sky upended and wide, and I feel like the loneliest person in the world. But I prefer this, if I'm honest, to the strangers who elbow me on the tube, to the insincerity of small talk at work, to my mother's chatty roll of one-sided conversation tinny down the telephone. Because it's here, alone, that I can mourn you, in silence, in secret.

Sometimes I lie down on the hard wooden floor and I look up through the windows and from down here, I swear I can see where the world curves; the very edge of existence. I look at the few loose stars rolling like spare change in the city sky and I wonder where you've gone and why. There are some days when I begin to surface from sleep, the morning still only a violet crust, and I think I can smell you, the bitter but not unattractive trace of sweat lingering in your crevices, the nooks in which I used to cradle myself. Feral, I sniff you out in the corners of my own skin, taste you in the glue of my raw morning mouth. My palms feel in the half-light for the solid wall of your starry-moled back before I remember that you're not there.

I wonder if this is how she felt, the young widow walking under the moonlight desperately looking for her love match, her soul locked inside some gnarly, silvery tree. Sometimes at night I wake up startled, and I'm not sure if it's you haunting my dreams or her.

*

I wish I could say the last person to have touched me was you but it was the policeman who came to tell me your body had been found, collapsed face-down in a heap, pale grey like dirty snow, still in your reflective running gear somewhere off the uphill track that leads to the neglected fountain at the top of Alexandra Palace. As he spoke, the policeman looked down at the floor and then he put his hand on my left shoulder and squeezed it, hard. 'Sorry for your loss,' he said.

It was only after he had gone that I remembered how my mother used to say that we all have an angel on our left shoulder who records the bad things we do. I imagine my left shoulder angel now, holding a scroll as vast as an overspilling ocean, listing the minor details of my life and the major ones too. I wonder if touching the widow's tree is in there, held against me since I was thirteen, along with sleeping with you all these years when I wasn't even supposed to be alone with you in the first place.

*

According to the holy book, widows are not supposed to leave the house, especially not pregnant ones. Sometimes I think that was her mistake, the widow under the tree; she ought never to have been out walking in the first place. If only she'd stayed home, like she was supposed to have done. Pregnant widows, like us, like me and her, aren't supposed to leave the house until we 'lay down our burden'. This is exactly what the scripture says, what the scripture calls it: a burden.

When I first read this particular line in my copy of the holy book that my parents gave me when I left for university, and instructed me to keep on the top shelf, higher than any other book, I wondered if it was a misprint, an error in translation. I imagined a centuries-old scholar with ink-stained fingers, smudging his cursive with his thumb in a slip of studious exhaustion, leaving later generations to fudge his intention and read between the lines. I thought it might have been a mistake because a burden sounds much the same as a punishment, as though this is all my fault, as though I am the one careless for losing you, and this to me seems surely a mistake.

But I ordered three other translations off the internet just to check and they all say the same.

A burden it is then. At night the taste of cold copper slicks my tongue and sour water lurches from my stomach in alarmingly violent spurts. I feel sick all the time but there's nothing left to throw up any more. I'm six weeks or seven, I forget now, for I've lost count of time. If only you'd stuck around; I was planning to tell you later that day.

*

The thing is, though I wear the ring you gave me, except for the times I visit my parents and it lies hidden on a thin chain underneath my sweater, we were never actually married. We never did quite make it that far. It's not that we didn't want to be, you'd asked and I'd said yes and I meant it, I did, it's just that I kept putting it off. Talk to your parents, you said. They'll understand, you said. Talk to your brother, he's bound to be on our side, you said. But I wasn't so sure and so I let every opportunity to introduce the idea of you, if not yet the real you, pass me by. I always meant to tell them, I just never knew when and besides, you and I, we had so much time; we had the rest of our lives.

My family have no idea what I'm going through. I know what you'd say. You'd say, 'They love you.' You'd say, 'For God's sake, let them in.' But honestly, it doesn't matter how much I'm hurting. If I told them the truth, I'm pretty sure they'd be horrified.

*

In Catholicism, widows must follow a year of heavy mourning followed by six months of half mourning then six months of light mourning. In heavy mourning, a widow must wear black. In half mourning, clothes may be black and white or white and black. In light mourning, shades of lavender, grey and mauve are acceptable. In Hinduism widows are no longer forced to burn themselves on their husbands' funeral pyres, but there is an expectation of sorts that they will mourn their husbands' deaths for the rest of their small lives. In Judaism, a widow is forbidden from remarrying if she outlives two husbands who have died while she was married to them, the woman is considered as either having tremendous bad luck, which is not worth tempting again, or a malignant disease in her treacherous, murderous vagina.

My scripture says that widows should stay home, dress in plain clothes, rid themselves of jewellery and pretty things and make themselves blank, scrubbed off the page. It is easy for me to oblige. Since I spend all of my time at home, opening the door only for deliveries, I wear either my pyjamas or yours every single day. I've taken out the tiny diamond studs you gave me on our anniversary from my earlobes and I've twisted your ring off my finger with a fresh bar of lemon soap. Though not even so long ago I'd have railed against these prescribed erasures of a woman and her grief, it alarms me that I actually find some twisted pleasure in it. These rituals ask of me to forget myself and obeying the rules rubs the corners off me. It occurs to me that this willingness to comply, to do what I'm told, is what my parents have expected from me my whole life.

Sometimes I look in the mirror, my face tear-stained and tired, and I wonder why the hell I'm doing all this. I mean, I'm not even your widow, strictly speaking, at all. Though I keep up the pretence in front of my parents, I stopped believing in God a long time ago, and so technically, I don't have to obey the scripture anyway. If I wanted to, I could leave my flat, I could wear make-up, I could throw a goddamn party and celebrate your life with a slideshow full of photos of us projected on the wall. There is nothing making me do any of this. But I feel like your widow because you were the one I loved. And for some reason, the rules of the religion I inherited the moment I was born seem to anchor me in my grief, my grief as deep as a glassy sea, which I fear I might otherwise drown in. They give me a strange sort of reason to be.

*

My parents are religious in a sort of superstitious way. They write 786 in birthday cards, sip holy water and shudder at the sight of an upturned shoe. Whenever my brother or I leave after a weekend's visit, they hold the holy book high over our heads, to bless us on our way. 'Nazar na lage', my mother always says, so as to not tempt fate. There is though, I guess, only so much she can do.

My parents' house is covered with glassy evil eyes, blue like a spring sky, hanging on hooks above doors in unexpected corners. When I moved into my flat, my mother presented me with one, a garish painted eye with its pupil slightly off-centre as though drunk. She'd bought it from a Turkish butcher in Turnpike Lane while buying meat to fill up my freezer and she held it up to me, dangling it like prey from her fingers. 'To protect you,' she said. It hangs on my living room wall. The first time you saw it, you startled. You always found it a ghastly menacing thing, refusing to kiss me in front of it; taking it off the wall whenever you could only for me to put it back up again just because. One morning, I put it on your pillow just to tease you and the fright it gave you; oh, my.

It's still there, on the wall. Maybe I should have taken it down a long time ago. One thing I've never understood is why, if the eye is supposed to protect me from evil, it's called evil itself. Did it bring bad luck here, into my flat, did it spread it to you too? Because, really, who dies when they go out for a run? When have you ever heard of such a thing? But then I remember that gnarly tree, and the widow, and I remember that she only went out for a walk and look what happened to her. She was face-down too, just like you, and I don't know if I'm going mad, and I don't know why, but I just can't help but think of her. Did I do this to you? Did she do this to me? Or did my mother's evil eye?

\*

My mother calls and says it's been too long since I've visited so she insists I drive up from London for the weekend. A part of me is scared, not because she might notice anything but because of the rules; I'm not supposed to leave the house. But she insists and I don't have the energy to argue and besides, I tell myself, the rules don't even strictly apply to me. I remind myself it's just superstition, that's all.

When I arrive, she's in the kitchen cooking a feast and though at first I'm not sure if I can stomach anything and have no idea how I'll get through all this food, suddenly hunger rages through me. I feel as though I've not eaten for weeks and that part probably is true. I linger in the kitchen while my mother asks me briefly about work and comments on the shadows under my eyes and then continues talking about herself. She chops and steams and fries, filling me in on all the details of suburban life, bemoaning the traffic and the lack of parking, recounting her latest dinner party, naive and oblivious to my pain.

After dinner, my mother pushes back her chair and returns with my favourite pudding in a terracotta dish, an elaborate concoction of creamy rice swollen in sweet milk and sprinkled with pistachios and dried rose petals that takes hours to prepare, and she presents it to me proudly as though I'm here for my wedding, not merely a weekend. 'You've gone to so much trouble,' I say, because I know she's showing she's made an effort for me, and she touches my face and says, 'Every time you visit, it's so special.' In that tiny moment she is so gentle that I want to believe her and I wish I could tell her everything about us, about you, about what's going on with me.

But then she turns to flick the kettle on and she starts talking about some random girl I sort-of grew up with who, it turns out, is now apparently living in London with an Irish guy and it seems that this is the talk of the town among my mother's friends. She goes on and on about it, what a scandal it is, what a shame, and she shakes her head as she squeezes the teabags one by one, pitying the girl's mother while also implying she must have done a bad job in the first place, to have raised her to be that way.

I listen to her witter on, saying how glad she is that I didn't turn out like this other girl, how grateful she is for a daughter like me. That's when I realise there's really no point in telling her about you, about us, about everything. It's far too late now. You're gone and even if I could tell her everything, where would I begin? What would I even say? In her eyes, everything I have done, everything we had together, is a wretched sin.

*

Back home, I can't stop checking my underwear. There's a part of me that knows it's going to happen, that can already sense our unborn baby was always meant to be an impossibility. And then I see it, under the blinding strip of the bathroom tube light: the first rusty smear of old blood the size of my thumbnail.

I curl up on the living room floor under the window and I wait for the rest. I watch the lavender clouds move slowly like thin shadows across a forlorn face. I'm aware that something terrible is happening inside of me; there is such pain, it makes me roll. The stars look like pennies scattered in the sky, and for some reason, in my delirium, I think of that gnarly tree I touched so many years ago, the bark silver like the moon, and I think of unborn babies crying and hair pinned into the earth, tangled in the soil, and I think of you, face-down in the snow, and I feel as though I have nothing left in me. In a moment of clarity, I realise the crying I can hear is coming from me. At some point it is over, it is done. I've laid down my burden as your not-quite widow and with it, every last trace of you is gone. I sense something watching me and then I see it glinting on the wall, my mother's evil eye shimmering as bright blue as a warm ocean. It occurs to me, a few nights later when I'm calmer and warm in clean pyjamas, after it is all done and I am cleaned up, that no one in my family will ever need to know about you, about us, about this baby that never was. People say things happen for a reason; in my family, they call it kismet or God's will. Is this my kismet, I wonder? Was this really how it was supposed to go? Am I cursed or am I saved? For years, I will wonder this. For years, I will never exactly know.

# Foreign Parts

Spots of damp perspiration pop through Mark's shirt as he swallows the smoggy night's heat, clutching a paper bag that Amina asked him to hold tightly to his chest in order to give his clammy hands something to do.

He stands behind her, patient yet awkward, while Amina argues with the shop seller. The shop seller, plump and short, is showing her several thin shawls spun of wool as fine as silk, which fall weightlessly like the paper wings of dead moths as he shakes them out, but Amina is argumentative in her mother tongue. Mark does not know what she is saying but he hears a sarcasm in her laugh that he has not heard before, a ring of clipped spite that chimes her class, her confidence and her self-assured status before this man, who merely sells shawls. Amina is not like this in London, he silently observes.

Mark is not like this either. In Lahore, he lacks purpose. There is little for him to do so he stands behind Amina, holding her shopping or one of the numerous handbags she has suddenly acquired, feeling passive and uncomprehending and of no real use. Lahore is not like their week in Rome, when Mark read to Amina aloud from their guidebook every morning over cappuccinos and cornetti, affecting an Italian accent to make her laugh, her lips flicking flakes of sweet pastry everywhere. It is not like their weekend in Paris, when Amina reached out for Mark's hand and he led her over the Pont de Sully, deftly shunning the Left Bank for the Right, winding her this way and that through quiet, unpopulated streets with the expertise he'd so proudly gleaned in his gap year so many years ago. It is not like the time they walked through the Lake District one damp autumn, their route studiously plotted by Mark the night before while Amina soaked in a pedestal tub in their luxury bed and breakfast. Lahore is not like that at all, he thinks. He has shown her many places and many cities, holding them open and unfolded for her in the palm of his hand like a pop-up greeting card for her to stroll about in next to him, both of them side by side. But Mark does not know Lahore. He cannot place himself in it like a cardboard cut-out. He can show her nothing here and he waits for her instead, to lead him and talk for him in an unknown tongue he cannot decipher. Only she does not.

She is at ease here, in the city where she was born and brought up. She does not look to Mark for directions and nor does her hand slip into his the way it usually always does in London or wherever they have been, where they loop arms or her fingers search for his inside his pocket as if inside their own little magnetic field. It is not because they are careful with their affection in this different city, this different place; on the contrary there are couples, hand in hand, everywhere. It is because Amina is different here. Sometimes Mark thinks she has simply forgotten he is there.

'Chalo,' Amina says abruptly, her hair a straight dark sheet swinging at her shoulders. 'Let's go,' she orders, stepping straight-backed and empty-handed towards the door. Mark follows.

It is dark outside, but her sunglasses still push back her hair. The shop seller is scooping up his fine, feathery shawls one by one. Now he must fold them all again. He shakes his head with a sorry smile and a chubby shrug to Mark as if to say, Women. Mark nods and presses his lips inwards together by way of a wordless reply, following Amina out the door, the paper bag holding the beaded flat shoes she bargained half an hour for, even though the original price was one she could more than easily afford, still clutched to his chest.

Outside, the humidity rises all around him, bursting in his face like an overfilled balloon, and it hits him once more, a sudden, tight ache binding his entire body. He is relieved when Amina tells her driver to take them home. In the backseat of the car, she curls her legs underneath her and rests her head on Mark's shoulder, but it is too hot for him still and her knees press into his uncomfortably. He shifts. She looks across at him and sits upright instead.

In Lahore, Mark reads gestures, not guidebooks. He reads privilege in the nonchalance of Amina's family's casual stance as they lounge on their sofas every afternoon wearing thin, cool linens when the tea trolley, wheeled by the kitchen boy, comes out like clockwork. He reads expectations in Amina's father, as he invites Mark into his study for a sip of bootlegged wine to chat about how much a deposit for a house in London might cost. He reads stiffness in the driver and the maids who never quite meet his gaze. He has nothing to do, and he reads the unspoken words around him and wonders why he is here at all.

Most of all, he reads Amina. She is a new edition in Lahore, a volume untouched. She smells new. She is shinier and more polished here in her family house, with its immaculate lawns behind high gates, than she is in their small, rented two-bedroom flat in west London. There, they casually brunch on weekends, eating toast without plates in crumpled nightclothes covered in crumbs. Here, Mark observes, she is always pristine, her face poised and made up, while she waits impatiently for the maid to fill her china cup with weak English breakfast tea. They spend every day together, but she is further away from him here than she has ever been. There is a self-importance that Amina carries, along with the designer handbags that she has suddenly rediscovered in the walk-in closet of her teenage bedroom, that Mark has not seen in her before and it bristles against him uncomfortably.

It was Amina's idea to come to Lahore. There were people she said she wanted Mark to meet, relatives and friends, and places she wanted him to see before their wedding. But when they met her old college friends at the Gymkhana members' club for tea, she left him aside, launching into high-speed conversation in a voice he had never heard her use before. It was only after he jostled her elbow and gave an awkward laugh that she took him by the arm like a child and brought him forward to introduce him, but even then he felt ignored. At numerous family dinners hosted by her rich relatives in honour of their engagement, where he has worn stiff, starched kurtas that itch at his neck, he has stood shifting on his feet, unsure of who to speak to while Amina laughs loudly over some comment some guest makes instead.

Mark wanted to see the Pakistan of the photospreads in his *National Geographic* magazines but he has seen it only from the backseat through the car window as the driver takes them from markets to shopping malls and back home again. He has seen street children in torn clothes peer in, leaving marks on the window where their hot breath and their raw fingertips have been. He has seen old withered men polishing shoes at roundabouts, faded Afghani turbans wrapped around their heads. He has seen tailors hanging dyed silks out to dry in oranges and pinks and reds to make clothes for new brides. He has seen glimpses of all of these people and all of these things from his place on the backseat but when he poised his camera ready to capture them, Amina laughed at him and sneered and said, 'Honestly Mark. What is there to see? They are so dirty. I would not want pictures of them.'

*

In Lahore, Amina is changed. In London, they stay up late watching *Newsnight* and *Question Time* and listening in earnest to debates about social change. He had thought these things mattered to Amina as they did to him, for at home they share the Sunday papers and listen to Radio 4. But now he has seen the house where she grew up, grand and gated with its marble floors and mod cons, and he has watched, faintly disgusted as though swallowing a resurfacing aftertaste, as she scolds the maid for not ironing the crinkles out of her silk clothes or for making her tea too weak, and he feels as if he does not know her at all, under the layers of privilege that, he assumes, she must have missed greatly, for she has taken to it all so effortlessly. He wonders whether she is really happy in their tiny rented flat back in London. He wonders which Amina he will marry. This one, or the one he left behind.

Mark and Amina have planned a small wedding in London for early next spring. Mark was proudly prepared to pay for it all, budgeting carefully and creatively. Amina talks about the wedding most afternoons with her mother and her mother's friends and her old friends from school, but she never mentions to them the things she had discussed with Mark before.

Instead she talks about venues, fancy hotels and exclusive social clubs that he has never heard of at all. He overhears Amina suddenly considering expensively draped marquees, illuminated and airy, laid out across immense grounds, and sees her flick through glossy magazines pointing at thin pouting models wearing elaborate designer Pakistani gowns. This is entirely new to him.

Amina is entirely new to him, spoilt and demanding like a child with an ungentle mouth. 'Maybe,' she says, mulling over a bridal spread in a magazine on their last night in Lahore while Mark repacks their suitcase, 'maybe we should marry here, Mark, in Lahore, instead.'

It is not what they agreed. Mark says nothing for a moment and hesitates before saying he had thought she had wanted to marry back home in London, and what about their plans for that? 'Your home, or mine?' swipes Amina, standing square as if to pummel him, a speck of spit shining on her lower lip like a fleck of sugar or salt. Mark is not prepared for this. He is not prepared for a fight, for it happens so rarely. They have always agreed on everything before.

Amina is in tears now. She is shouting at him, about not understanding her and not making an effort with her family and her friends. She is shouting at him about how now he must know how it feels to be her when they are in England, left on the outside looking in. She is shouting at him about how ridiculous he has been, waiting for people to talk to him, when he should have spoken to them first. She tells him, spitefully, that people have laughed at him in Urdu; her poor, aimless English fiancé lost in Lahore. She tells him he has embarrassed her, just sitting there, saying nothing to no one at all. She tells him to look around and to notice all of the things that she has here, all of the things she has given up to stay in London with him instead.

Mark has never heard her say anything like this before. It had never occurred to him that she might feel as self-conscious in London as he has been here in Lahore, and he wonders whether it could possibly be true. He wonders whether to say something, about how she has been changed here, how he has found her hurtful and haughty and cold, only he does not know how. He is weary of the heat and of the humidity and of the effort being here requires, even though, really, with all the maids and the drivers there is no effort required at all, and he is ready, so ready, to go back home.

So he sits on the bed, with their unpacked suitcase at his feet, and he lets Amina shout and he lets her cry for he knows that tomorrow they will finally leave. It has been a long fortnight, he consoles himself silently in his head, and later, when they finally fall asleep, he tells himself it is only these foreign parts that have disjointed them, and nothing else. He tells himself Amina did not mean what she said. He tells himself that she was just tired, and he thinks of how when they land in London, she will reach out for his hand and they will slot back together once again.

On the flight, which they sit through mostly in silence, Mark flicks through the few photographs he took. No, he thinks. Lahore was not like their week in Rome or their weekend in Paris, and he deletes the photos, one by one.

## Too Much

Amal had sent an email to Shaheen a day earlier, a few lines saying only that she would make her own way home from the airport and expected to arrive at six o'clock in the evening, signing off with her initials AMC above the formality of her email signature, which she had so excitedly set up on graduating – *Amal Martha Copeland, BA Hons, English and Philosophy, UCL* – instead of a kiss. Shaheen read nothing into this brevity for she had grown used to these short rare notes appearing sporadically in her inbox. It didn't matter any more. Her daughter would be home for dinner for the first time in nine months. She told her colleagues at the radio network where she worked: Amal is coming home in a month. Amal is coming home in a week. Amal is coming home today. They had never been apart this long.

Shaheen had taken the day off work to prepare. Though the cleaner had already been earlier in the week Shaheen cleaned the house once more with a chirpiness unlike her, humming along to the songs on the radio, listening to the same talk show she helped to produce. In Amal's room she laid fresh sheets and left a small brown box tied with a cream ribbon on her desk. It contained a thin gold chain with a tiny horseshoe pendant the size of her pinky nail, which she had purchased last year at a Christmas market in Muswell Hill, the first Christmas Amal had not been home, the sort of gift Shaheen knew Amal would like, the sort of gift she hoped would last for ever. She had filled the bathroom cupboard with expensive lotions, made sure to purchase the coconut-scented shampoo Amal liked so much. She glanced at the clock over and over.

She had booked a haircut for the afternoon not just in anticipation of Amal's return but because she needed a cut and a colour and had the day off work anyway. It was nothing drastic, a few inches trimmed to bring her hair above her shoulders and slivers of pale grey strands painted chestnut again, but when she looked at herself in the mirror, she saw someone brighter than her years. She stopped at the organic food market near the train station on her way home to pick up all the ingredients she would need to make Amal's favourite meal; mushrooms and garlic and a pot of thick cream to toss with fresh ribbons of tagliatelle, sharp bars of chocolate that she melted and folded and baked into brownies. She planned to cook the pasta after Amal arrived, perhaps while she took a bath. She waited. Amal must have landed by now. She would be on her way.

Shaheen could not wait to spend some time reconnecting with Amal again. There was so much she wanted to know; about Spain, about her course and her future plans, about whether there had been anyone special while she was away. There were things she wanted Amal to know too, like how while she had been away, Shaheen had made more of an effort to join Lisa and her other colleagues for after-work drinks and had even been on a number of blind dates. The dates had come to nothing, but they had been fun and in their immediate aftermath, she had longed to phone Amal and tell her about them, laugh about them with her. That was the sort of relationship they had; best friends, not just mother and daughter. She knew Amal would have shrieked with excitement about the dates. Although there had been other men since Ralph, there had been nothing and no one steady enough to last longer than a few months at a time and Amal had been telling her mother for the last two years at least to take it more seriously and date online. Before Amal had left, Shaheen stood in her doorway watching her pack and when she asked only half-jokingly if she could call her every day Amal laughed, 'Mum! You'll have all your newfound independence! You'll barely notice I've gone!', which Shaheen took to mean no.

A week into her yoga training course in a remote village in southern Spain, Amal had emailed Shaheen and after describing her room and how wholesome the vegan food was, she explained that the teachers had asked them to stay in the present moment, focus entirely on their higher sense of self and keep distractions to a minimum. 'It matters to me that I make the most of this opportunity. So I won't be able to keep in touch quite as much as usual. I will email when I can. It's a good lesson in switching off – something to discuss for your radio show!' She explained then that they were handing their mobile phones over and that they were only allowed to check them once a week. At first Shaheen was dismayed. The course providers should have told the students this beforehand. But when she looked up the website for the Paz Yoga Retreat, it was clearly stated in the FAQs. It was then she realised Amal had kept it from her, had not wanted to make leaving harder by telling her they would not be able to talk while she was away.

Even when Amal went to university she still lived at home with Shaheen, taking the tube every morning from Archway to Russell Square. It had been Amal's idea and though Shaheen had never insisted she was relieved when her daughter said she did not want to live in university halls, that she did not see the point. 'Besides,' she told Shaheen. 'Think of the money I'll save if I just stay here,' although they both knew it was not about the money at all. Ralph had left when Amal was just a little girl and though it had been a long time since Shaheen had prayed, she routinely whispered into the atmosphere and touched the knots of wooden tables and chairs in gratitude for a daughter as considerate, as caring as Amal. She had sometimes wondered whether she had done the right thing, being quite as open with Amal as she had been about Ralph and showing her sadness and her loneliness over all of those years, those nights spent crying on the bathroom floor, which she wondered now if Amal could still remember, but Amal had turned out beautifully. 'She's a saint. You know, she's more like a best friend than a daughter,' she often told Lisa. Lisa, who had three teenage boys, sighed and told her how lucky she was.

Though life became looser when Amal started university, less grounded by homework and fewer evenings spent at home just the two of them, Shaheen still felt grateful for her presence in the small terraced house in Whitehall Park into which they moved after the divorce settlement came through. Sometimes she would be reading in her room or planning production notes for the network's afternoon shows when she'd hear Amal's key in the door, the soft thump of her bag falling to the floor, and it was as comforting to her as the warmth of her bed. After her own strained upbringing Shaheen vowed to never force curfews or stringent rules or religion on her daughter and it astonished her that Amal was so sensible and gave her so little cause for concern despite having the freedom to choose to do whatever she wanted to. Amal was vegetarian and didn't drink. She preferred doing yoga and going to feminist literary talks in Gower Street to clubbing and parties. Shaheen had worried that Amal might have grown up wary of men because of Ralph, because of the things Shaheen knew she had said, but throughout the first two years of university she had a steady loving boyfriend, a philosophy student named James. Their relationship ended with a maturity that startled Shaheen; James and Amal remained close friends. Sometimes she felt ashamed thinking of all the times Amal had heard Ralph and her fight, screaming how much they hated one another, how they wished the other dead in front of their only child.

At the airport, Shaheen threw her arms around Amal and cried even though she had promised both Amal and herself she would not. 'I'll miss you so much,' she gulped. 'Please call me! I know you'll be so busy, but please, if you can?' But Amal held her mother's hands and said, 'Mum, this is important to me. It'll be good for you to have a bit of a break too. Okay?' Shaheen nodded, between small wet sobs and downturned smiles, and after Amal passed through security, Shaheen sat uncomfortably on a hard plastic seat in departures for twenty minutes, her hands over her face, crying softly.

Later Shaheen wondered what Amal meant by 'having a break,' as though they were an obligation to each other of some sort, but then she shook her head at the absurdity of this unkind thought. Her daughter was too good for that.

*

Shaheen waited until 7 p.m., an hour after Amal had said she'd be home, before calling her. It went straight to her voicemail, which she noted had been updated to include a Spanish greeting as well. She assumed Amal was still underground on the tube from Heathrow. But her flight had landed on time and she should have been here by now. She called again and again but Amal was still not picking up her phone and now Shaheen began to worry. She pulled out her laptop, bringing up contact details for the yoga retreat. Perhaps she had missed her flight, perhaps she had lost her phone. She would not panic. She would call the retreat first, they would know. When a man eventually answered Shaheen was already flustered, pacing the living room.

'Oh yes hello, buenas noches, I'm looking for… I… do you speak English?' and she laughed nervously when the man said yes. 'Thank God, I wonder if you could help me. I'm looking for my daughter, Amal, Amal Copeland? She, um, she's been at the retreat for… months, nine months, on a training course and she was meant to come home to England today and I've been waiting for her. She should have been home by now but I haven't heard from her, do you know if she checked out on time?'

The man laughed a little, deep and syrupy but not unkindly. 'Madam, we're not like a hotel, we don't do checkouts,' he said. His accent was European with an American roundness; she was relieved to find she could understand him.

'Oh, okay, I'm sorry. What I meant was – did she leave on time? For her flight? I'm just, I'm worried. She's not answering her phone and I wondered if she missed her flight, if anyone knows?'

'Well, let me reassure you,' he said. Though his English seemed fluent, he spoke slowly with a sing-song tone and this bothered Shaheen. 'Amal is fine. She's staying here for a little longer. In fact, she's going to be working for us now that she has her yoga accreditation. She may not have had access to the computers or her phone to let you know earlier but you don't have to worry. She is fine. I just saw her myself and she is happy.'

Shaheen stopped pacing and gripped the back of a dining chair. When she spoke, her voice was low and thick, and came from somewhere fleshy at the back of her throat. 'What do you mean, she's "working for you"? Where is she? She's meant to be home, right now. I want to talk to her, I want to talk to her now,' she demanded.

'I understand you are concerned, but please let me reassure you that she's fine. I saw her myself just a half-hour ago,' he said, speaking with a steadiness that Shaheen found patronising. 'Right now she is in evening meditation and our retreat rules prevent us from interrupting practice.'

'Are you kidding me? Your retreat rules?' Shaheen lost it. 'I want to speak to my daughter, now!'

'Mrs Copeland, I must ask you to calm down.' The man spoke louder now.

'I need to—'

'I can have her call you tomorrow.'

'I'll fly out tonight—'

'You can talk to her tomorrow.'

'No, now!'

'Mrs Cope—'

'My name is not Mrs Copeland!' she shouted finally. He sighed. 'It's the best I can do. The best I can do.'

Shaheen could find nothing else to say. She sat back down, slumped into the hardwood dining chair, her forehead hot and heavy in her cold palm. The man continued in his slow, syrupy voice once more. 'Amal wanted to stay here. We offered her a job. She did not want to leave. You must respect her wishes. You must put her first.'

'Put her – what are you saying? What has she told you? I always put her first.'

'Tomorrow. She will call you tomorrow. Namaste.'

The line went dead.

Shaheen was sat with her head in her hands when her phone beeped with a message. It was Lisa wishing them both a lovely evening, asking Shaheen to give Amal her love. Shaheen threw her phone at the wall and, later, poured the thick cream for the pasta sauce down the sink, stuffed the brownies in the bin.

*

Shaheen told everyone who asked that Amal had a last-minute change of plan and was staying on in Spain for longer, a sort of extended gap year working as a yoga teacher before looking for graduate jobs back in the UK. Lisa, who was the closest person she had to a best friend, was the only one she eventually confided in.

'I've been wondering,' Shaheen said as they sat drinking on high stools in a stuccoed wine bar around the corner from the network's studios, 'if I did the right thing. Everything that happened with Ralph; it was my pain but I made it ours. Perhaps it was too much. Perhaps I ought to have protected her from it more. She was just a little girl. I mean, every time Ralph had her on weekends, I didn't hide how that made me feel. She grew up knowing my hurt, knowing how badly it went wrong.'

'Shaheen, you've said it yourself, she's a saint. As far as rebellion goes, yoga is hardly worrying. She'll be home soon,' Lisa said. 'You've raised her beautifully and most of that you did on your own. You should be proud of her. Proud of yourself. She needs space, that's all.'

The yoga was supposed to have been just for fun; a distraction post-graduation, time to think about what sort of career she wanted to have. Shaheen had offered to line up internships and introductions at the network and often told Amal that with her clear voice and natural way of drawing people out and putting them at ease, she had what it took to be a presenter or a broadcast journalist, but Amal seemed uninterested despite so many of her friends wanting to work in the media. 'I don't want it to look like nepotism,' she said. 'I want my job to… mean something. Maybe charity work or an NGO. I don't know yet.'

Ralph worked in corporate finance and Shaheen often referred to him as an ugly capitalist beast. Shaheen, who had worked hard for years to reach a senior role in production at the network, despite its tendency to favour Oxbridge graduates, retorted: 'My job means something. At least it's not like his!' and Amal said quickly, 'Mum, that's not quite fair.' But before Shaheen could say anything else, Amal moved on and mentioned how she'd been thinking of pursuing yoga more professionally.

'It's so much more than just exercise,' she said. 'The philosophy behind it. It's so enlightening. So spiritual. It makes me feel so at ease, so complete. I feel it's something I've been missing. You know?'

Shaheen did not know. The truth was she found Amal's passion for yoga, which first started back in sixth form and had since grown into a daily habit, a little silly. But she never said this to Amal, of course, because she had always promised herself that she would let her daughter be her own person and make her own choices, whether big or small, unlike her own parents who punished her for falling pregnant outside of marriage by eventually cutting her out of their life. They had insisted Ralph marry Shaheen, which Shaheen had hoped would win them over, but in the end it was not enough. So when Amal told Shaheen she wanted to train as a yoga instructor and that she had found a course she liked the sound of in a converted farmhouse in Spain, Shaheen didn't talk her out of it. It was just an adventure. She swallowed her criticisms and concerns that Amal might miss out on better opportunities after graduation, and instead paid for her yoga training, insisting on upgrading her accommodation to a single room with an ensuite so she might have some privacy, spending a small fortune on sleek yoga leggings from an expensive Hampstead boutique. She did all of this because when she was pregnant with Amal, she whispered to her unborn daughter that she would be the sort of mother who would let her child be free, that she would not bind her child to her by blackmail or guilt, which was the only sort of mothering Shaheen herself had ever known.

Amal did not call the next day but she did write her mother an email three paragraphs long sent at dawn. 'MUM!' she wrote. 'I'M SO SORRY!!!' as though she had only forgotten to pick up milk on the way home. She explained that she had packed all her things and was about to leave the retreat for the airport when Eduardo, the man Shaheen had spoken to on the phone, surprised her with a job offer. 'Just like that!' she wrote. The idea of being paid to do something she loved as much as yoga was an opportunity she couldn't turn down, she said. But by the time she had unpacked and moved into her new lodgings in the staff quarters, she had missed access to the computer room, which was locked for several hours a day. She didn't explain why she didn't phone.

'I hope you're not too upset,' she ended. 'I know you were expecting me home and I hope you didn't go to too much trouble for me. But like I have said before, this matters to me and I feel it is important that I put myself first right now. I'm finding myself thinking a lot, reflecting about my past, making plans for my future. This is something I need to do. Does this make sense to you? I hope you can understand. I appreciate your support and everything you have done for me. I'll stay in touch when I can.'

There it was again, this need to put herself first. 'But I have always put you first,' Shaheen wanted to say. 'What point are you trying to make?' she wanted to reply. But Shaheen could not reply because every time she sat down to, she felt confused and bewildered, her fingers trembling. Amal used to send her mother messages while she was at work, signing off with 'Love you!' But she was as distant as the moon now and Shaheen didn't understand. It took Shaheen weeks to respond and in the end all she wrote was simply, 'What did I do?' She never did receive a reply.

Months passed. She kept the door to Amal's bedroom mostly closed for she had no reason to go in. Once, after the cleaner had left the door ajar, Shaheen stepped forward to pull it shut again and noticed the small brown box holding the horseshoe necklace still sitting on the desk. Shaheen swept it into a bin liner along with other old things she no longer had a need for.

*

Shaheen booked time off to fly out to Spain even though Lisa tried to talk her out of it. 'You don't want to make a scene,' she cautioned. 'You don't want to be that sort of mother. She'll come back to you, you'll see.' But Shaheen couldn't just wait and see because she *was* that sort of mother, how could she not be, and because when it came to it she wasn't entirely sure with her whole heart that Amal really would come back to her after all. 'I have to try,' she said to Lisa.

After she'd booked her flights and found a hotel, Shaheen considered calling ahead and leaving a message for Amal to tell her she was coming, but she remembered how patronising Eduardo, the man she had spoken to, had been the last time. Besides, she couldn't shake the dreadful feeling that if Amal found out, she'd try to stop her or simply find a way to not be there when she arrived.

On the plane Shaheen was restless, her knees and her feet jiggling as though a low electric current was running through her legs. She sat at the very edge of her seat caught between feeling excited, as if she'd planned a huge surprise party that was just about to start, and physically sick from worry, bright white spots appearing every time she closed her eyelids and tried to sleep. When her flight finally landed, she was grateful she'd had the foresight to book a car with a driver to take her to the yoga retreat because in this state, she would not have been able to concentrate on the road. Her driver appeared to have spent his entire life under the sun, his face and hands the colour of an almond skin and just as wrinkled too. He smelt like cigarettes and wore a leather jacket on top of a white tee-shirt even though the outside temperature was nearly thirty-two degrees. He introduced himself as Manuel and tried to make small talk in English but Shaheen quickly put a stop to that, with her pursed lips and her forehead pressed against the window. In the car, Shaheen fell into a daze and then a deep sleep, a yellowing landscape of dust passing her by as her anticipation turned into an exhaustion that crept up on her. Three hours later, she awoke with a start just as Manuel turned off the engine and said, 'Lady, we arrive.' She felt caught off-guard, her mouth dry, aware that her saliva tasted sour and her breath smelt like stale bed sheets. She ran her fingers through her hair. 'Thank you,' she said. 'Please, could you wait?'

Outside the ground was dry and the air heavy and fragrant with the scent of purple and yellow wildflow-ers crowding a dirt path that led to a tall gated fence. Shaheen pressed a buzzer beside the gate and waited. Nobody came. She pressed the buzzer again. She glanced over at Manuel with an apologetic, weak smile but he raised a hand and pursed his lips as if to say, it's fine, there is plenty of time. Fifteen minutes later a young man, a boy really, dressed in white baggy trousers and a pink tee-shirt, came running to open the gate. He was out of breath, spoke quickly in Spanish, gesturing at the farmhouse behind him, only just in sight.

'I'm sorry, I don't understand,' Shaheen started. 'English?' The boy shook his head. She pulled out her phone for Google Translate but nothing loaded up; she turned to Manuel, who was leaning against the car, smoking a cigarette. She shrugged at him helplessly and then Manuel dropped his cigarette, squashed it with his shoe and strode towards her.

'Manuel, can you please help?' she said, looking between him and the boy. 'Could you please tell him, I'm looking for my daughter. Amal. A-M-A-L. Tell him I've come from England and I haven't seen her for so long; I just need to see her.'

'I understand,' Manuel nodded and then turned to the boy and passed her message along. Shaheen gasped when the boy said, 'Ah, Amal, sí, Amal.'

'Sí, sí, yes, Amal, my daughter,' she said, tapping her chest with her hand in a gesture that meant, she's mine, she's mine. The boy continued to speak and shrugged his shoulder, while Manuel's voice rolled in return; Shaheen recognised only the word 'Gracias', which Manuel said as the boy turned and ran back up the path. The gate in the fence shut tight behind him, the lock clicking into place.

'What did he say? He's going to fetch her for me?' she said, her voice trembling like a butterfly or a bee.

'He's going to see if someone can come,' Manuel said. His face was thick with creases and not unkind. 'She has been here long, your daughter?'

'Nearly a year,' Shaheen nodded, searching for her sunglasses in her handbag, as she bit her bottom lip. Manuel said nothing. He walked back to his car and returned with two plastic bottles of warm water. 'Gracias,' she whispered. She sat down on the dirt path, not caring about her clothes. Manuel hovered, walked in large circles, stretched his back, checked his watch, his phone.

'I'm sorry,' Shaheen said, 'thank you for waiting. I'll pay you for your time.'

'When you are ready, I am ready,' he said. 'No rush.'

The gate opened again and Shaheen scrambled up on to her feet. The boy was back, not with Amal but a man instead. The man was older, skinny with a shaved shiny tanned head. He wore thin white trousers bunched up at the ankle and baggy round the legs, just like the boy's, and a grey tee-shirt with 'Paz' on the front in a typewriter script. He smiled at Manuel, then Shaheen, and pressed his hands together in prayer in front of his chest.

'Mrs Copeland, we spoke some months ago on the phone,' the man said. 'Eduardo,' he added, pressing his hand to his chest by way of introduction. 'Welcome to Paz, our home of peace.' He bowed his head. All these yoga manners; Shaheen didn't know what to do in return. So this was Eduardo, she thought. She immediately felt her chest tighten.

'Yes, hi. I'm not Mrs Copeland actually; I'm Amal's mother, my name is Shaheen Khan, and Copeland is Amal's father's surname; but anyway that doesn't matter,' her words spilled, breathlessly. 'Look, I've come to see my daughter. I need to see my daughter,' she said. 'Please, Eduardo, can you take me to her? Or can you bring Amal to me? Can you tell her I am here? Can you? Please, it's very important.'

'Has there been a death in the family?' Eduardo's question was so direct, it threw Shaheen off-guard.

'What? No; I just, I haven't seen her in months, nearly a year now, or spoken to her and I—'

'Amal has embarked upon a silent, meditative journey. We can only interrupt her silence if something very critical has happened, like the passing of a loved one. And even then, it is not something we can do immediately. We must wait for the right time. Though in this case, I understand, there is no crisis?'

Shaheen felt her knuckles form a fist; it was all she could do not to punch this man. She cleared her throat, but still her voice came out darkly, thickly.

'The crisis, Eduardo, is that you are holding my daughter here. You have held her here for nearly a year. I need to see her now, or I swear I will call the police.' She clenched her phone.

Eduardo said something in Spanish to the boy. Then in a calm and poised tone that only served to make Shaheen feel even more irrational, he said in English,

'The police do not come here, Mrs Cope— Mrs Khan. Paz is a place for peace. It is a place for meditation. Amal, she came here to find peace. I can assure you I am not holding her here. She is here by her free choice. She is not ready to leave, so what can I say? Had you called to let me know you were coming, I could have saved you a wasted journey.'

Shaheen, astonished, looked from Manuel's face to the boy's back to Eduardo's. 'It's not a wasted journey. I will wait here. If this is a "home of peace", the least you can do is invite your guests in.'

Eduardo bowed his head once more. 'We invite all of those who come here to participate with great hospitality. But we have rules concerning visitors who are not here for yoga, for reasons of security and space, and so with regret I cannot let you in. You are very welcome to wait, as long as this kind gentleman,' he gestured to Manuel, 'does not keep your meter running so long that you run out of money!'

'Security concerns? Space? What are you even talking about? There's plenty of goddamn space,' she said, gesturing wildly at the stretches of fields around them, the farmhouse far off in the distance, 'just let me in!' Shaheen pushed her hands onto Eduardo's chest, and at the same time Manuel stepped forward to intervene and Eduardo put his hands up in the air and backed away and said, 'Woah, woah, no; that is not okay.'

Somewhere in the commotion, Eduardo shut the gate behind him. 'You may come back tomorrow, Mrs Copeland, sorry, Mrs Khan, and we can have the same conversation again. But Amal will not see you. What she is doing is a great test of endurance. You should be proud of her dedication, not angry about it. The best I can do is write a message for her. But I have come to know Amal very well and she is very committed, and I do not think she will want to break her meditation. I cannot make her and I am sorry, but I do not want to either. This is something that is important to her and you must respect that. Goodbye, Mrs Copeland; Mrs Khan. Namaste.'

Eduardo bowed and turned away with the younger boy by his side and Shaheen watched them retreating through the fence. They didn't look back. In that moment, she was so overcome that before she knew it, Shaheen was sobbing into Manuel's tee-shirt, breathing in the smell of cigarettes and leather in little gasps in between. At some point, he put his hand lightly to the back of her head.

On the way to the hotel, Manuel offered Shaheen his assistance for the duration of her trip. The next morning, he collected her at 8 a.m. and drove her back to Paz, where a variation of the previous day's conversation played out at the gates with another member of staff before Shaheen gave up and he drove her back to the hotel again. Manuel drove her back and forth like this for three days. Eduardo did not come to the gates again; it was always someone else who couldn't speak

English. Back at the hotel, Shaheen passed the rest of every day in a state of suspended shock, numbly flicking through television channels and ordering meals she forgot to eat before writing emails to Amal that oscillated violently between being either incredibly angry or incredibly apologetic, begging her to come home. Amal didn't reply. At night, it took her hours to fall asleep but when she eventually did, she was so exhausted she did not stir until morning. On her last day, the plan was for Manuel to take her to Paz one last time before going on from there to the airport. He was about to take the turning that led to the retreat when Shaheen reached out and touched his shoulder and said, 'No, no need. Straight to the airport, please.'

Inside the terminal, she changed her flight for one to Paris instead. She had already decided she would do this two days before. She could not bear to go back to London, not yet. Going to Paris on a whim was a liberty she could afford; she had earned a promotion, after having spent so many endless nights since Amal had left working late in the studio to avoid coming back to a lonely, empty house. While she waited for her new flight, she booked herself, indifferently, into a luxury suite in a five-star hotel off the Champs-Élysées just because she could.

*

In Paris, she felt as though the world was spinning around her. On her first night, she woke startled from a dream in which she saw herself walking into a vast road, straight into an onslaught of screaming traffic. On her first day she ventured out for a walk but turned around again, overwhelmed by the noise and the bright lights of all the flagship stores screaming for attention. One night she stayed up watching a film from her bed and it wasn't until the end credits ran that she realised she hadn't taken in a single thing about it; even two minutes later, she could not have told anyone who the main character was if they had asked her. Another evening, on her way down to the hotel spa, she passed a yoga class taking place and she stopped to observe through the doors. She wanted to smash the glass, tell them how ridiculous they all looked.

Shaheen had spent some time in Paris many years ago as a student herself, before she met Ralph. She had not been there long, a month at most, as part of a summer exchange scheme through her university. She had mostly forgotten everything about that short trip, which had taken much persuasion and a personal letter from her university tutor addressed to her parents for them to finally agree to let her go, but as she took dinner alone in the hotel's ballroom she considered for the first time that here she was again, in a foreign place, all alone. Every holiday she had ever taken, everywhere Shaheen had taken Amal, everything Shaheen had ever done; all of it had been for Amal, to show her the world, to make her feel loved. 'I feel it is important that I put myself first right now,' Amal had written. 'But I have put you first your whole life,' Shaheen had wanted to say. For the first time here in Paris, away from the home that she had created with and for Amal, away from the city in which she could not help but search for the back of her daughter's head in the crowds emerging from the underground, she realised that there was no need for her to think about anyone else. Across from her table, a young, dark-haired man caught her eye and smiled at her with a hesitation she found naive. Her hair was shorter now and she had lost the extra weight she had been carrying, not by specific effort but because she found it time-consuming to cook for nobody but herself. There was a glittering coolness in her eyes where once a softness had been and her face had hardened, her cheeks now hollow and defined where once they had been plump, but she was aware that this lent her a certain air that she supposed some men found attractive. Somehow, because she was lonely and angry but mostly because she wanted to remember what it felt like to be in control, she let this young man buy her a drink and then two and then she let herself guide him back to her suite upstairs by the hand. She let him move into her. She let him take her again and again and again first until she felt something, then until she felt nothing at all. When she stirred at daybreak, she noticed the young man was still there, fast asleep.

She covered her mouth with her hands, in horrified disbelief, and then she shoved him with her foot, woke him and told him he had to leave. But though her voice was trembling with rage, she was unable to yell, and could only manage angry-sounding whispers.

On the flight back to England later the same day, Shaheen stared blankly out of the window and slumped in her seat, avoiding eye contact with the little boy in front of her who kept turning around and trying desperately to engage her in a game of hide and seek. The boy's mother showed no air of being irritated by him and seemed rather on the contrary to want to encourage his playful behaviour, lapping up compliments from other neighbouring passengers on how cute he was in a way that Shaheen thought was pitiful. The child insisted on turning around, again and again, the tips of his pink fingers peeking through the seats. Shaheen resisted the urge to pinch them or swat them away with the inflight magazine, as if they were little fat flies. Finally, she stared at him without smiling. Her mean expression frightened him and after that, subdued, he left her alone and Shaheen felt awful, then.

As soon as they landed, she checked her phone for messages but still, there was no word from Amal. The next day, Shaheen called in sick to work claiming she had food poisoning, eventually returning the following week full of bright little white lies about how wonderful her holiday had been in spite of her sickness, which she offered to her colleagues when they asked how her trip was. When they asked after Amal, she said with false exuberance, 'Oh you know. Having the time of her life.' On occasion she elaborated, adding enthusiastically: 'It's all so beautiful over there, I don't blame her for not wanting to come back to London.'

She only told Lisa the truth, that Amal had not wanted to see her, that Amal had not replied to any of her messages. 'I don't know what to do,' Shaheen had said, struggling to finish a sentence, each word a pebble in her throat. Lisa threw her arms around Shaheen but Shaheen just stood there, her arms heavy and hanging by her side, and the embrace felt awkward and unwelcome. Lisa looked at her sympathetically with tears in her eyes, which only made Shaheen feel worse. All Shaheen could think of was that Lisa had a husband and three teenage boys while Shaheen had nothing and she could not even say why.

*

For months, Shaheen moved forgetfully. She frequently missed a tube stop or a bus stop or ended up headed in the wrong direction with no idea where she was going. If she went shopping, she found she could not remember what it was she needed or why she had gone into that particular shop in the first place. She felt often as if the world around her was spinning and she wondered if this was what it was like to be concussed. A blow to the head, to the heart; that was what it felt like, Amal's absence.

Sometimes, Shaheen thought of that night in Paris with the young man whose name she did not even know. She remembered how, for that night at least, it made her situation more bearable. She tried to recreate that feeling. One night, she slipped into a hotel bar alone after work in the hope that she might meet someone who was just passing through, and though she was approached by a man, and though he looked as though he might have kissed her, she felt self-conscious and uncomfortable. In the end, she made an excuse and the man sneered after her as she left and thanked her in a sarcastic way for wasting his time. She hit her forehead with her hand and asked herself repeatedly what the hell she was doing, feeling only a deep sense of repulsion at herself. After that, she oscillated wildly between telling herself righteously that she was fine on her own, that she did not want or need anyone, not even Amal, and then crying so much at her own loneliness that her head hurt as if it might burst from bewilderment.

Finally, the following spring, she was invited to Lisa's house for a barbecue. It was there that Lisa introduced her to Philip, a family friend, who was divorced and lived alone in a big house in Crouch End with two elegant Russian Blue cats. He smiled at Shaheen pleasantly and said, 'I've heard so much about you,' which made her cringe but also blush. All afternoon, he stayed by Shaheen's side, or if they parted and Shaheen ended up talking to someone else, he found a way to come back to her, offering her a glass of something sparkling or holding out a bowl of dessert. From time to time, Lisa glanced across at them encouragingly. In the bathroom, Shaheen stared at her reflection and considered the alternatives and realised that there were none she preferred. By the time she'd emerged from the bathroom and walked back across the lawn, she had already decided: she would throw her heart to Philip, and hope that he might catch it. Philip suggested a walk through the park as they left and it was easy to accept.

She was so tired of the large emptiness that echoed around her and he paid such attention to her. The more time she spent in his company, the more she realised how much she had missed affection, the simple gesture of a man's hand reaching out for hers, his fingers touching her elbow or the inside of her wrist or the small of her back, and these tiny moments alone were enough to move her to tears. Philip was gentle with her. Over time, he offered her a domestic routine punctuated by normal, small things that made her life feel complete. He opened his front door for her before she found the keys he had given her at the bottom of her handbag. He cooked for her, plates of comfort food, thick soups and heavy roasts, and at night he held her in her sleep. Shaheen did not immediately tell him about Amal because she feared if she did, he might find her unbearable too. When eventually somehow it came up in conversation, he sighed deeply and said, 'I always knew a piece of you was missing.' For some reason, this made her want to be with him more.

Once, when Philip had gone away for a week for a conference, Shaheen found herself alone in his living room, curled up on the sofa phoning Ralph for the first time in years, despite the fact that they had long ago agreed that their correspondence would only ever be through their solicitors. But it felt somehow urgent to Shaheen to ask him the questions she was dreading, which were: 'Have you spoken to her? Do you know where she is?' For the longest time, Shaheen had dismissed the idea that Amal might ever choose to talk to Ralph over her, for the idea seemed absurd. Shaheen and Amal were a team, they always had been; it had always been them against the world. But that was before, and now the only thing that Shaheen felt sure of was that she didn't really know Amal at all. Ralph didn't pick up and Shaheen was relieved she only had to leave a voicemail. 'Ralph, it's me, Shaheen. Look. I... I don't know if you know, I'm sure she must have told you, but Amal's in Spain and... I'm having difficulty reaching her. I just, you know, just wondered if you had a number for her. Or if you'd heard anything. Let me know. Okay. Thank you. Thanks.'

Ralph didn't call back but he sent her a brief formal email a few days later, somewhat confused. Amal had left Spain and was settling into a new job in

New York, moving in with her boyfriend in Brooklyn. 'Didn't she tell you?' he asked and it seemed to Amal that perhaps there was something smug in his tone, a feeling she wished to recoil from. It took a few days for it to sink in; that Amal was emailing Ralph, *Ralph*, that she was telling him what was going on in her life but not her. When it did sink in, Shaheen was alone in Philip's house, in the sunlit kitchen, sipping a glass of water, when she suddenly dropped it and found herself hanging onto the kitchen island, falling to her knees, a fleshy cry escaping from the back of her throat that sent the cats scattering, wide-eyed and frightened.

Eventually Shaheen moved in with Philip. She braced herself for emptying out Amal's bedroom, fearing it would be just too painful, but in the end she felt nothing; it was just stuff, that was all. At first, after Amal stopped replying to her emails, Shaheen used to sit in front of her laptop and search for her online methodically, but all of Amal's privacy settings were high. She continued to email her on every birthday, long letters in which she was careful not to sound spiteful, but then by the third year she simply wrote: 'I hope you are happy, wherever you are, whatever you are doing,' and after that she wasn't sure if she'd keep writing any more. Once she thought about emailing James, to ask him if Amal had ever told him anything that might have explained more explicitly this need to put herself first, to push her own mother away, but in the end she realised that perhaps it was just one of those things that happened, like the turn of the moon or the swell of the sky or the way some nights the stars disappeared entirely behind the clouds. In a way Shaheen had done this to her own parents too, as much as they had to her, and though she had long ago stopped believing in God, sometimes she questioned if this was fate's cruelty or revenge. There was so much she misunderstood, so in the end she concluded that maybe Amal was not as happy at home with her as she had assumed. Maybe Shaheen had been too much. Maybe she had depended too much on her daughter, to be her everything. Maybe Amal was happier without her. Maybe in the end, it really was as simple as this.

Shaheen set up a search engine alert with Amal's name, though she rarely ever received updates, certainly never anything that gave her personal life away. Once Amal's name appeared on a list of attendees at an international yoga summit in California; another time on a hotel review in Montreal. But that was long ago, and it was all Shaheen had ever found. She checked in with Ralph once or twice over the years with thinly veiled excuses she was sure he could see through; she'd say elaborate things like how her email to Amal's address had bounced back because Amal's inbox was full or there'd been some problem with the server at work and her inbox had magically emptied itself and she'd lost all of Amal's messages but all she wanted to know was: had he heard from her? Was she okay? When he told her, always briefly, that he had, and that she was, her heart didn't break quite as much any more, perhaps because it was already broken, perhaps because it was enough to know that at least Amal was alive, that she was doing just fine without her.

Sometimes she found herself googling private investigators, always snapping herself out of it by the time she'd landed on their Contact page. At times it felt impossible to Shaheen that Amal had hardly any presence online, a thought that simply sat there in the back of her head waiting to be examined. One Sunday while Philip cooked lunch, she tucked her knees up beneath her on the sofa, her laptop in front of her and a glass of wine on the coffee table, intending to read book reviews online while the cats lay by her side, but she found herself on Google. This time, instead of typing in 'Amal Copeland', a small idea came to her to use Amal's middle name, the name Ralph had always preferred. They had argued about her name before she was born. Amal's name was a sort of gesture that Shaheen had bestowed upon her at birth, something to connect her in some small way to a tiny piece of Shaheen's past, though Ralph didn't see the need. She didn't know why she hadn't ever thought of it before; it was so obvious. And suddenly, there she was. Martha Copeland.

Martha Copeland's life was still highly private, still protected behind the boundaries she had left north

London for, but there were at least little clues; her lovely face and her lustrous brown eyes shining from within the small circle of a profile picture on one site, her head resting on a handsome young man's shoulder in another, her name listed as a director of wellness at a popular women's networking collective in New York. Shaheen observed Martha Copeland and studied the pixels of her face, a woman now, not just a girl fresh out of university. She felt a strange sensation of falling through her thoughts, through her body, feeling her heart beating under her skin as though any minute now, it might stop. *So this is who you are*, she thought. *This is who you are now*. She didn't cry; she didn't request to follow or become a friend. But she couldn't stop herself from reaching out, touching the tiny circle of her daughter's face, as though picking up a tiny fleck of a crumb with the tip of her little finger. From the kitchen, Philip called to say lunch was ready. She shut her laptop and slid it away. The cats curled around her legs. *Amal.* It had meant hope or something like that; but Shaheen guessed that maybe it didn't even matter any more.

# Waterlogged

It was the first time they had been away since before the baby was born. Shona shivered. The bed and breakfast was grand, an old Georgian house set three storeys high, but everything about the house was old and inefficient, especially the rattly heating. Shona pressed the backs of her thighs against the thick cast iron radiator under the window in the dining room, but the warmth was thin and barely creaked through her jeans. The back of her neck and the tip of her nose felt as cold as Fireworks Night. She was dying for an extra-hot coffee, to wrap her hands around it. But she was still breastfeeding and coffee was just another thing she couldn't have, high up on the mental list of sacrifices she had made.

At three months Raffy was not a good sleeper, unlike the other babies born to the women in her NCT group, who seemed to sleep satisfied like milk-filled kittens all through every night. On the worst nights, Harun read aloud to her from his phone about how even the smallest amount of caffeine could pass through a woman's breast milk, leaving a baby restless and awake for hours. 'Are you sure you didn't have a coffee today?' he asked her suspiciously whenever Raffy awoke, as though there could not be any other reason for his nightly distress. Some days, when her caffeine cravings were as strong as a kick to the skull, she scoffed at the research and surrendered. Once, she drank three black Americanos and that night Raffy woke eight times. She pictured dark spots of glossy espresso percolating through her watery breast milk, the colour of pale butter, into her baby's soft hot mouth.

Last night, Raffy had been up six times and she hadn't had a coffee for nearly two weeks.

Harun held Raffy curled up like a conch shell over his shoulder while making animated small talk with Gregory, who owned the bed and breakfast with his wife Liza. Gregory was a tall man with a flourish of white hair. His cheeks were shiny like baubles. Broken veins crept along the sides of his long thin nose like spiders' legs. Shona smiled a thin line in the general direction of their conversation and then turned around, her back to them. She looked out of the window like a bored child as they discussed Brexit the way people now did in everyday conversation, as mundanely as they did the weather. Outside the sky was the colour of a silver coin, tarnished at the edges. The rain fell in flat cold sheets. It was just their luck, Shona thought.

'Right then, what can I get you? Coffee? Tea?' Gregory asked, rubbing his hands together to signal the conversation moving on.

'A coffee would be grand, thank you,' Harun said brightly. Shona was still looking out of the window, her back towards them, and so Gregory did not ask if he could bring her anything.

*

A fortnight ago, Shona had taken Raffy to a sensory class with some of the women from her NCT group and as their babies writhed on their backs like sea creatures watching bubbles float by, the others talked about their plans for the coming Easter bank holiday weekend. Ellen and Rob were going down to Devon to stay at Ellen's sister's cottage. Suzan's in-laws were visiting from Edinburgh and had offered to babysit so that Dan and Suzan could go out for dinner on Good Friday. Lydia, who waited for everyone to share their plans first, announced that she was going to Paris. Ollie had surprised her with tickets, she said, and had even booked her in for a series of treatments in the spa of the luxury hotel where they were staying so that she might have some time to herself. Everyone cooed, both at their babies and also at this, collectively marvelling at the thoughtfulness of such a husband, considering that such a husband might exist, although Shona couldn't help but wonder what it was Ollie might have done wrong. Pleased by the appropriate responses, Lydia wore her satisfied smile like a fake-fur coat draped over her shoulders.

That night, over takeaway pizza for dinner in front of the television, Shona suggested to Harun that they go away for the Easter weekend too.

But Harun frowned, unconvinced, peering at the football results on his phone.

'I don't know, Sho,' he said, 'It sounds stressful. He'll be up all night and then you'll be even more tired. We'll just be paying to be exhausted somewhere else.'

'Lydia's going to Paris,' Shona said, without looking up from her slice. 'Ollie's booked her into some spa so she can have time to herself.' She rolled her eyes.

'Good for her.'

Shona's eyes felt as thin as paper from sleeplessness, as though if she rubbed them too hard they might accidentally rip apart, leaving her vision patchy and piecemeal.

'I thought it might be nice, that's all,' she said. 'You know. Change of scene. I'm not talking about a big holiday. Obviously. Just a weekend away. We don't even have to go far.'

The next morning before he left for work, Harun said, 'You know what, you're right. It'll be good for us to go away. Let's do it. Let's go someplace with our little guy. You'll have time to sort it out, right?'

When he bent to kiss her goodbye Shona turned away because she had not yet had a chance to brush her teeth and so he only caught the very corner of her mouth.

*

Gregory and Liza had lived in Oxford for forty years. Gregory was a retired professor of history who had taught at the university but who now spent his time researching and writing academic books while Liza took care of the bed and breakfast business. Shona had found their house last minute. She had been searching for cottages in the Cotswolds, picturing a sleepy little thatched cottage in a pretty village, but everything she looked at had already been inevitably booked up months ahead. Then Gregory and Liza's townhouse popped up in a page of search results showing rooms still available.

When Shona mentioned in her booking request that they had a three-month-old baby, Liza offered them the large double bedroom with its own bathroom across the hall that spanned the entirety of the top floor. 'It's the biggest room,' she wrote, 'so you will have plenty more space for the travel cot and there's less chance of the other guests being disturbed!' She added, 'We love babies, we have five grandchildren of our own!'

In the photographs the bedroom looked stately, with large sunlit Georgian windows and a king-size bed piled high with cosy throws. There were two dusky pink armchairs and in the corner, an antique writing bureau. The bathroom had a black and white chequered floor and a roll-top bath under a sloping ceiling. 'Lydia can have her spa,' Shona said to Raffy, who looked up at her expectantly from his bouncer seat, stretching his legs like springs, while she sat in front of the computer. 'This will be fine for us.'

The morning they were due to leave, the spring sky turned pigeon grey and Shona's heart sank as she retrieved Raffy's waterproof all-in-one and rolled up her raincoat. She asked Harun, 'Have you even done your packing yet?'

Harun didn't look up from the paper. 'It'll take me five minutes, max,' his mouth full of toast. He flicked through his phone. 'Looks like rain,' he said, 'oh well.' He took another bite.

*

The waterlogged clouds finally burst on the motorway, rain pounding the windscreen like hard fists. Shona wondered if it was raining in Paris, decided it probably wasn't. Raffy had fallen asleep within minutes, rocked by the hum of the car. Harun took work calls on his Bluetooth as he drove, occasionally lifting his left hand off the gearstick or the steering wheel to cover Shona's while continuing to look straight ahead at the road. All the way to Oxford it rained hard and flinty, the sort of rain that didn't seem to stop. Shona looked out of the window, following the raindrops as they slipped into each other and snaked down like racing tadpoles.

'Hey, you're quiet. What's up?' Harun asked in the silence between his work calls.

'Oh, nothing,' Shona replied. She didn't have the energy to point out that he was not even talking to her anyway. She rested her head against the window, wondering if she ought to try to sleep.

'Guess we'll be staying in then, if this rain doesn't stop,' Harun said.

An hour later, they pulled into a gravel driveway on a quiet residential road. Liza flung open the front door as Harun parked the car, a cloud of dazzling, daffodil-yellow hair standing on the steps. 'Welcome! Welcome!' she shouted under the cover of the porch as Shona and Harun dipped their heads in and out of the car and under the cold rain. Shona scooped Raffy out of his car seat while Harun opened the boot, hoisting bags over his shoulder.

'Hello, welcome! You must be Show-na,' Liza said, ushering her into the large hallway. 'Have I said your name right?'

'Hi, yes, I'm Shona,' she said, without correcting the mispronunciation that she had heard all her life. 'This is Raffy, and that's my husband, Harun.' She gestured to the car.

'Ha-run,' repeated Liza, 'Like Aaron, I see. What lovely names you all have!'

'Right, that's all of it,' Harun said, shutting the front door. He held out his hand for Liza to shake, as though meeting a client for the first time.

'Lovely, lovely,' said Liza, smiling widely. 'Good journey was it? Pity about this ghastly weather. Well let's get you settled in then, shall we?'

*

'How's he doing?' Harun said, sitting on the edge of the high bed, kicking his shoes off and nodding in Raffy's direction.

'Just needs a feed,' Shona said, sitting on one of the dusky pink armchairs. She lifted her top up and flicked the clasp of her maternity bra with one hand. 'Are you cold? I'm bloody freezing,' she said, shivering under the coat she was still wearing as she clasped Raffy to her.

All of a sudden, seemingly out of nowhere and for no reason at all, Harun clapped. One big loud boom. Raffy's eyelids flickered and his fists unfurled, startled. When they first met, Shona considered this, the way Harun signalled a subject change with a giant clap of his hands, a modulation as alarming as a large balloon ruptured by a needle, an odd, nervous tic, but then she realised that Harun didn't get nervous and it was a long-term habit, an annoyance she had to put up with that still made her jump. She closed her eyes. 'So,' Harun said. 'We're here now. So what do you want to do? Any rainy day plans?'

'I guess after Raffy's feed, we can go find someplace nice to eat?' Shona suggested. She stroked Raffy's cheek. Harun walked to the window and pulled back the lace blind with one hand like a spying neighbour.

'It's coming down pretty heavy now. I don't know, I don't think I fancy taking Raffy out in this. Let's stay in. Go out tomorrow,' he said. He looked up suddenly. 'Did you bring my raincoat?' Shona shook her head. Harun bent down and took his laptop out of his bag.

Shona felt Raffy swallow gulps larger than his mouth could contain. She stuck her little finger in his mouth, breaking the grip of his wet gums. She stood and held him over her shoulder, rubbing his back. In front of the window, she swayed. With her other hand, she peeled the delicate lace blind back, watching the raindrops collide into each other again and again.

*

Gregory came back into the dining room carrying a tray with two mugs of coffee and a large bowl of pale scrambled eggs. 'Get stuck into this, then!' he said, a wide grin slicing his face in two. Shona noticed his teeth were the colour of wet sand.

'Help yourself, help yourself,' he said, gesturing towards the four different types of cereal that had been tipped into large blue and white porcelain bowls covered in clingfilm. Milk had been poured into a matching jug. Shona moved towards the table, thinking that perhaps Gregory had brought that second coffee for her, and that perhaps she might have it too. Gregory reached forward to pull out a chair. Just as Shona was about to thank him Gregory sat down opposite Harun, reaching for the second cup of coffee himself.

Liza called from the kitchen. 'Darling! The toast's ready! Bring the tray!'

'Right-o!' Gregory groaned as he stood back up again. 'Coming!'

Shona pulled out the chair next to Harun instead. 'Is he really going to have breakfast with us?' she murmured, leaning towards Harun, stroking Raffy's small head.

'Why not? It's his house,' Harun shrugged. 'Nice guy. Friendly. Huge house!' he said. He passed Raffy over to Shona and helped himself to half of the eggs, glancing around the large square dining room. An imposing mahogany dresser took up the entirety of one wall, filled with dinner sets and cut-crystal glasses. Framed family photographs covered every available gap; a set of small blond-haired children gathered around a Christmas tree or on a beach and then a row of smiling graduates in mortarboards. The dining table was vast, large enough to seat twelve. But there were, it seemed, no other guests.

Gregory returned with the tray laden with thick triangles of white toast and pots of sticky jams. He sat down opposite Harun and their conversation on London property prices resumed. It turned out that their eldest son lived in west London. Gregory mentioned that all of their four children had attended Oxford University and Shona could see Harun was excited, his eyes shining like blisters, itching to mention that he himself had gone to Cambridge. But Gregory kept talking. 'Personally, and I mean no offence, but I find London a ghastly place,' Gregory whispered dramatically, leaning forward. 'I tell my son as much also. But mark my words, just one weekend in Oxford, and you'll be hooked. Even in the rain! Excellent schools for the little chap, too,' he said, reaching for another piece of toast, and nodding in Raffy's direction. 'And the university too, you never know.'

Shona could tell this was Harun's cue to mention Cambridge, but just then Liza came in with a shiny pot of tea. She wore a cream apron covered in pastel polka dots over a thick jumper and a corduroy skirt; she looked, Shona thought unkindly, like a housekeeper. 'Oh Gregory,' Liza chided. 'He's always trying to get our guests to move to Oxford. I keep telling him, if you end up convincing everyone to live here, then there'll be no need for our B&B!'

Everyone laughed tinnily. Liza pulled out another chair and sat down herself.

'I hope you don't mind us joining you,' she said, beaming at Shona and Harun. 'Only we do so like to get to know our guests, don't we, Gregory. Tea?' She looked around at all three of them with the hopefulness of a primary school teacher.

'Please,' Shona said, pushing forward her mug with one hand, the other clasped softly around Raffy's back.

Gregory looked up in surprise, as if he had only just noticed her.

'Goodness! I didn't even ask. And what will this little chap have?' Gregory asked, waving a piece of toast in Raffy's direction.

'Oh, he's fine,' Shona said. 'He's only three months old, he's not on solids yet.' Raffy was staring out at the thin grey daylight filtering through the window, trying stoically to hold his head up like a puppet on a string, bumping his chin on her shoulder every few seconds.

'Tush, Gregory!' said Liza. '"What will this little chap have," honestly! Look at him, he's tiny! Just a baby! You'd think he hadn't had four children of his own.' She raised her eyebrows and shook her head at Shona in exaggerated comic despair.

'It was so very long ago,' Gregory said, stroking his chin and chuckling. 'Liza did such a good job with them, such a very good job. So, now Harun, tell me more about the bank you work for. Harun here,' he elbowed Liza, 'works for one of those big American banks in the City. Like Geoff's son.'

'Is that so?' Liza said. 'Marvellous!'

For quite some time Harun talked about the bank and working in the City and then he in turn asked Gregory about his work at the university. Shona shifted Raffy in her arms as Gregory talked some more about the volumes of books he was working on, something to do with Soviet espionage. She briefly wondered if she might inch into the conversation, mention her own book, a novel about a marriage falling apart that was going to be published next year. She'd written it fast in a furious five months while pregnant with Raffy. Harun did not read fiction and he struggled with the novel, how it was written and what it was about, taking it badly at first. 'Is this meant to be us?' he asked Shona, an edge of disgust to his voice, and she covered his hands and told him no, explained that writing of the intricacies of relationships was something she had felt compelled to explore, that was all. The day she discovered her book was going to be published, she felt her heart skipping while Harun, who still did not quite understand why Shona had written the book or what an achievement it was that it would be published, explained to his mother on the phone that she didn't need to worry, that Shona's book was made up, an imagination, a hobby; it was categorically not about the two of them. Her book was already being talked about in the press, hints about her being one to watch, and she felt frequently as though everyone was talking about someone else, not her. But as she stirred her tea, she heard Gregory's voice still talking in long drones and in the end it was easier to say nothing than try to interrupt. She wondered if the rain might stop. She had hoped they might take Raffy out, find a restaurant for lunch while he napped in the pram. Yesterday they had stayed in their room all afternoon. Harun worked on his laptop while Shona sat with Raffy on the bed, half-watching television. She flicked through the book she was reading with one hand; she ate all the short-bread biscuits Liza had left on a tray. She fed Raffy for hours, clamping him to her breast, because there was nothing else to do. Later, Liza had come upstairs with takeaway menus for dinner, which they ate quickly in the front room downstairs. The evening moved slowly; the night more slowly still. Each time Raffy woke up unsettled, Shona slowly slipped out of bed, shivering while Harun turned in his sleep. The sixth and last time he awoke with his symphony of sighs and soft cries, she was too tired and too cold to try to settle him back in his cot and so she brought him back into bed with her, even though Harun never liked it when she did, calling it a bad habit like his mother did. In the end at around four in the morning, Raffy and Shona finally fell into a deep sleep together, Raffy curled up into her side like a baby bird while outside the rain continued to fall.

'And I suppose you,' Gregory nodded directly at Shona with his long, thin nose and Shona felt again that he had forgotten she was there, 'have got your hands full with this little fellow, then.'

Just then Shona felt something inside of her give way and because she was still so very cold and always so very tired, and because she simply could not help it and because she wished her husband might just say something just once to acknowledge what she was doing and all that she had done and because she also wished she had the strength to say something smart back to Gregory but knew she never would, her eyes filled to the brim with tears. 'Something like that,' she said quietly. 'If you'll excuse me,' she said, handing Raffy back to Harun. She pushed her chair back, and left.

*

Since Raffy was born, it seemed to Shona that time had stopped still and she could not shake the feeling that the world was spinning too fast, that she could no longer quite stand up straight. Time hung heavy over both of them. Every day she felt unnerved by how unreasonable her love and her fury, which had become one, seemed. She spent most days feeling stunned, aware only of a sort of rage swirling loose inside her like a rainstorm gathering speed, and it frightened her to think of what might happen if she were to let it implode. She was so angry with people, men like Gregory, assuming all she had was her hands full and that there was nothing more for her to show than the baby she adored, and she was angry with women like Lydia who made her feel like there must be something wrong with her for still wanting more. When Raffy was born, Shona was astonished by how thin he was. He was more pink than brown,

newskinned and slippery like a fish in her hands. Sometimes she was so overwhelmed by the details of him,
his violet eyelids, the waning crescent of his stomach,
the constellation of smudged birthmarks that spanned
the small of his soft back, that it brought tears to her
eyes when she least expected it. She adored Raffy with a
crushing force that sometimes frightened her. It wasn't
a question of her love for him; it was only that there
were other things about her too. She was terrified of
falling through the cracks and that no one, especially
not Harun, would even notice.

This new state of motherhood had left her unpre-
pared, foggy, slow. One of her biggest fears was that
her book wouldn't live up to everyone's expectations
and that even if it did, she still might not ever write
again. Where once she wrote as though the tips of
her fingers were on fire, staying up late into the night
after coming home from the newspaper where she
worked as a subeditor to write thousands of words
that she shaped into the book that was soon going to
be published, now she struggled to find the cadence of
a sentence. She pictured words and thoughts drifting
out of reach and then disappearing like snowflakes.
Some days she couldn't think of what to say to other
people, to the other mothers like Lydia and Suzan
from her NCT group or to Harun or the postman
or even to her own mother. She dreaded the publicity
she might be asked to do once her book came out and

she wondered if she might simply get away with being aloof, as part of her trademark style.

And then there was Harun. Some days she thought she hated him. Other days she looked at him objectively, with an indifference even, and she honestly had no idea how she had ended up with him. There was so much about him that she couldn't stand – his annoying phone voice, that god awful habit he had of clapping his hands to signal a subject change in conversation, the way he said things like how he didn't understand why anyone would bother to buy a newspaper when you could get it all for free online without realising what a big deal it was, for her to work on a national, to have made it that far and as a woman of her background too. It was not as if she had suddenly noticed this about Harun only since Raffy was born; she had known these things about him all along. But up until recently, she had thought she could bear it.

She had settled for him knowingly because she was so tired of being alone, of waiting for her situation to change. The truth was she had been in love with someone else for years, ever since university, but this boy, Leon, never took her seriously enough. She was never officially his girlfriend, merely his bookend, the one he came back to in between everyone else. Every time he drifted away again, she sat in her pale blue nightgown crying at the kitchen table while her housemates made her cups of tea, and told her he was a dick anyway, that she deserved better. Everywhere she looked, everyone else was getting married. One by one, her flatmates moved out to move in with long-term boyfriends who would sooner or later become their fiancés. When she finally told Leon that it had always been him and she asked him to commit, aware that she sounded like a teenage girl suggesting they go steady, he put his hands to the side of her face and said earnestly, 'Darling, let's talk about this tonight.' But tonight never came, because he never called and never again picked up his phone whenever she rang him. The idea of him was a fantasy; Leon would never have done what he'd have to do to be accepted by her family anyway.

In the end, oblivious to their daughter's heartache, her parents found Harun for her. Harun and Shona had known each other for eighteen months before Raffy was born; sixteen of those as husband and wife. He proposed, or rather his parents did, after they had met just three times, twice of those in the presence of their families, and a swift two-month engagement followed. After years of rejecting similar suitors, mostly because of Leon, Shona was swayed to marry Harun by the pros she carried in her head, all the things she felt ashamed of thinking about: at least he shared her background, at least he lived alone, at least she wouldn't have to move in with in-laws she didn't even know, at least he had a well-paid career that would comfortably take her away from her rented flat in Islington – which though it had been fun also made her terribly sad because it reminded her of how static her life was – into an entire terraced house near Alexandra Park. Sometimes she thought that she could love him, if only he toned it all down a little; if only he noticed the little things about her like how she liked to be held in bed or how she loved to have someone tuck her hair behind her ear or if he ever paid attention to the books she liked to read. Harun was not a reader; though he did concede that her book was certainly insightful (or that was the way he put it), he said he didn't have time for fiction. Of all the things about him, maybe it was this that Shona regretted the most; that he lacked imagination, that he didn't see beauty or poetry or the possibility of love in unobvious, subtle things. But Shona had known all this about him. She had accepted the certainty of this way of life, over the unknown of waiting for Leon to change. She had always thought she could live with it, that the stability of a family she could call her own would in some way make up for it, that she would change even if he didn't, but more and more, there were days when she was no longer sure.

*

Outside the air was plump, swollen with rain. Cold drops shimmered down on Shona's face, tingled with the salt of her tears. She had left her raincoat inside their room, high up on the third floor. She had not exactly intended to leave, it was only that she had heard what Gregory had said and she had felt the walls closing in. She hadn't really thought it through; their room was three flights up but the front door was standing right there, just as she came out of the dining room, offering a chance to slip away. If someone were to have noticed her right then, standing there trembling in the rain, if someone were to have asked her what was wrong, she might have grasped their arm for fear of falling. She might have told them that some days her sadness felt as unbearable as the end of a sort of beautiful film that left her heart aching and that what made it worse was that she didn't exactly know why because, you see, she had this baby, this beautiful perfectly formed baby, and she loved him so very, very much. Or she might have said that she had just needed to breathe, that she had just needed some space from her husband, that sometimes he could be a little intense, and then she'd have laughed it off with a shrug. Or else she might simply have said that she was just tired, just very, very tired, that was all. She crossed the road and stood at the corner of the street, not really knowing which way to turn. The road seemed endless, large stone houses that all looked the same set back from the road, windows covered with pleats of lace. Shona turned this way and that, but she could see nothing up ahead; this was not the sort of place she might find a café in which to sit and compose herself, gather her thoughts. Her hair soaked into thick strips that stuck to her face and she pulled the cuffs of her jumper over her wrists. She wouldn't stay out here for long, she knew that, she couldn't possibly. She knew that in a few moments, she would walk back to the bed and breakfast because it was raining, because there was nowhere else for her to go. She felt her nose running and wiped it with her cuff and at the same time, she suddenly felt the sensation of her breasts filling up with milk, as if by magic. Just a minute, she said to herself. She would leave in just a minute. But still, she looked around blindly through the rain, searching for someone to tell.

## Small Differences

Tasneem stood barefoot on the antique terracotta flagstones of the kitchen, grateful for their piercing coolness. Outside the heat was stifling. The air, unmoving, was pressing and making it hard for her to read and so she had offered to go in and make iced tea. Simon teased her for her inability to withstand temperatures over twenty-five degrees, as if her heritage somehow meant she was supposed to be immune. She pointed out the illogic of his reason – she had never lived in the Indian subcontinent, had not even been there since she was twelve – and then he softened, telling her he thought it was sweet, that was all. She stood up and stretched. It was too hot to come up with a retort, especially within earshot of his parents, so she had rolled her eyes at him and walked away.

In the shade of the kitchen, she pressed an ice cube to her forehead, her hairline clammy. She let it trickle down her neck and then began the tiresome process of opening each cupboard door to try to find the right sort of jug and remember where the tea was stored. After she had found what she needed and set the tea to brew, she searched the fridge and sliced up the last punnet of strawberries, eventually discovering a knife that was sharp enough in an overfilled drawer. They would have to buy more food and the thought of having to make an excursion to the village market with Simon's parents, of everything taking twice as long as they deliberated over what to buy and what to eat, irritated her. She told herself it was the intensity of the heat, that Simon did not ordinarily bristle her like this. But they had been in Tuscany for five days and, halfway through, their holiday already felt too long.

Tasneem heard the slap of Simon's flip-flops on the floor as he entered through the garden doors, but did not turn around. A few seconds later she felt him behind her, his arm warm around her waist, his face nestled into her bare shoulder.

'I'm sorry,' he said.

'You know, you're not that funny. It's hot. I hate it. Big deal. Okay?' Tasneem said, still without turning around.

'I'm sorry,' he said again and then he kissed her shoulder, spun her around and pulled her towards him. 'I love you,' he murmured into her hair and she let him hold her for just a moment but then she pushed him away.

'Too hot for all this nonsense too,' she said. Topping up the jug of tea with a blast of cold water, she tossed in yet more ice. She set the bowl of strawberries on a tray along with glasses and the jug and as she carried it out, she shook her head.

'Hey, let me,' Simon said but she had already stepped out of the door and set the tray down on the low wicker table on the terrace. Simon followed her under the shade of the veranda and lightly touched the small of her back, a gesture to show he would take over, and so she sat down on a worn sun lounger as he poured two glasses of iced tea. 'Here you are,' he said, passing a glass each to his father, his mother. His parents were talking about the weather, how they had not seen a summer so hot in the hills before. Tasneem waited but when Simon pulled out his phone to check a more detailed weather report, she poured a glass of iced tea of her own.

'Oh,' Simon said, looking up at her. 'Sorry sweetheart, I thought you had yours already.'

*

In the late afternoon, they drove to the farmers' market in the neighbouring town square to pick up supplies. Tasneem and Simon sat in the back and Simon reached for her hand, placing it in his lap like a teenager on a date for the first time, while his father drove and his mother sat in the passenger seat. It occurred to Tasneem as she looked out the window through her sunglasses at the passing scenes, the sunflowers edging the country lanes, the olive groves far off in the distance, that she had never sat in the back of her parents' car holding hands with a boy like this. From time to time Simon's mother twisted around in her seat to smile at them proudly and Simon squeezed her fingers a little tighter.

Upon arrival at the market Simon's parents planned a menu, counting off the remaining meals left to prepare for the week on their fingers. They ambled past stalls, taking their time to choose breads, cheeses and fresh pastas hanging in strips like shoelaces. In spite of her initial irritation at the idea of shopping, Tasneem found herself relaxing. The afternoon sun was still hot but the air was lighter now, the market livelier today than it had been before. The stalls were set out in the town square in the shade of a biscuit-coloured church, crumbling and spectacular. Today the church doors were unlocked and tourists wandered in and out seeking cool respite under its high holy ceilings. Stall-owners jostled with passers by, tempting them with ragged squares of bread to dip into sweet sharp vinegars, holding out small dishes of cubes of strong warm cheese and pitted olives to try. Tasneem marvelled at the size of plump tomatoes as large as the palm of her hand, took a bite out of a sweet, soft peach that an old man with a withered face almost as nutbrown as hers offered as a gift. Simon put his arm around her shoulder and she raised her hand up to meet his, their fingers clasped. They walked like this a little way behind his parents and for some time, as they sampled sugared almonds and crunched on grissini, swapping short kisses in between, Tasneem forgot the earlier annoyance she had felt towards him, not just today but all the other days since they had arrived in Tuscany as well.

Every night, Simon and his parents stayed up late as if he was home for Christmas, drinking wine and laughing over a set of family memories that were impossible for her to even begin to learn. 'Oh, it's a long story,' Simon said each time she tried to find a way into the turns of their conversation; or when he did try to explain, his mother or his father interrupted on a tangent and Tasneem was left on the edges again. Last night Tasneem had gone to bed early and as she brushed her teeth and heard Simon's father's rumbling voice and his mother's laugh so shrill creeping through the walls, she thought she might as well have not been here at all. But in the town square, they walked like lovers and Tasneem told herself that it was only the weather, prickling her skin and parching her mouth, that had been making her feel irritable like this.

*

When Simon first suggested they take a holiday together to Tuscany, it was a Saturday, late afternoon. Tasneem was frowning, her head bent over a cookbook as she followed a recipe for gnocchi. Her dough was sticky and she was worried the meal she had planned for their friends, who were Simon's friends, really, would be spoiled. 'You know, you could just buy gnocchi ready-made,' Simon said. 'It'd be much quicker, no one would know.' Tasneem flicked flour at him. Forty minutes before their guests were due to arrive, having boiled a fistful of dumplings and found them tasteless, Tasneem asked Simon to run down to the shop to pick up something else instead. She was disappointed and felt foolish. She had wanted to make a good impression on his friends. 'One day, we'll go to Italy,' Simon said in consolation. 'Eat all the gnocchi you like.'

Simon was not like any of the Pakistani boys she had been introduced to by her mother or her mother's friends. Ever since she had moved to London two years ago, phone numbers of strangers deemed eligible only by worth of their family origins and respectable jobs were passed along to her like Chinese whispers. She met them after work for coffee, sometimes making it as far as dinner, yet all the while uninterested in the stilted conversation she endured, resenting how much of her time her mother was making her waste. She had hoped that moving to London as soon as she had graduated, and starting a career, no matter how fledgling, would free her from the humdrum of her mother's expectations and the gossip of her mother's friends, and it angered her that it did not. When she met Simon at a book reading, he startled her first with his boyish preppy looks and his smart observations about the book they were there for, and then with the attention he paid to her; the way he smiled at her and laughed with casual determination as he asked for her number before he left. It took him a day to ask her for dinner and two more dinners until she slept over in his bed. They fell into the rhythm of an early love: lie-ins on Sundays and cosy dinners midweek, texts and emails all day when they were apart at work in opposite ends of the city. Sometimes when she least expected it – while unpacking groceries or sitting on the sofa choosing a boxset together, or reading in bed next to him, her head resting upon his bare shoulder, his fingers softly stroking her hair as though lightly strumming an instrument – she felt a sharp sting in her heart, a stab of worry, wondering what her mother would think.

Simon brought Italy up again after their friends had left, while they stacked the dishes together. He told her his parents had a summer house in Tuscany, an old villa with a postage stamp of a swimming pool set high in the hills, which they sometimes rented out for the holidays. It had been some time since he had last been. He said he would find out when the house was vacant, certain his parents would not mind. 'We'll be lord and lady of the manor,' he said, 'it'll be just us.' Tasneem felt a thrill and she curled into him as they both studied the calendars on their phones, choosing potential weeks in the summer they could ask for time off from work. She did not yet know what excuse she would come up with to tell her mother, who thought Tasneem worked late three times a week when, really, she was sleeping over in Simon's flat in Holland Park opposite a bookshop, to which he had quickly given her a key and a shelf within his wardrobe. That night, as they moved towards each other in bed and Simon murmured about all the beautiful places in Tuscany he wanted her to see, it never occurred to Tasneem that she'd ever feel as though she didn't belong with him, certainly not under the warmth of the sun in a place where the fireflies danced at night and the scent of lavender hung low in the air.

*

At the other end of the town square, Tasneem spotted a table crowded with baskets of books, antiques and bric-a-brac. She left Simon on the church steps and told him she would come back in ten, twenty minutes. 'Take your time. I'll wait here,' he said, although she had already turned away. The stall was covered in curios; stacks of second-hand books spilling out of fraying baskets, a bowl of swirled glass marbles, an intricate jewellery box carved from wood. These were the sort of treasured, artful things she saw scattered in the houses of the girls with whom she went to school, girls whose parents were writers and composers and artists with the stability of an inherited wealth that provided them with large houses full of hardback books and private education for all of their children. Tasneem, on the other hand, had worked hard to win a scholarship and her own childhood home was uncluttered and functional. Simon, who also favoured an organised interior and stacked his books neatly behind closed doors, at least had this in common with her mother. But Tasneem was drawn to this chaotic, expensive world of artistic curiosities like a moth to a filament. She smiled at the stall-owner, ran her finger along the rim of a delicate milk glass, light and pale as a pearl, held a crystal bowl in her hands, complementing its cut details. The stall-owner was pleasant, settling into an easy conversation with her, a light Italian lilt to her English. Tasneem lingered, passing her hand over a basket of books and was surprised to discover one she had long ago meant to buy, and here it was in this little market, a nearly new copy of the *Penguin Book of Italian Short Stories* translated into English. 'My goodness, I've wanted this for ages,' she said to the stall-owner. 'It's meant to be.' She smiled as she paid and thanked the stall-owner for her time in shy Italian, and then she looked back across the square to the church steps. She squinted but she could not see Simon there. It suddenly felt urgent to her to find him, show him the book and share her excitement in discovering it here; to acknowledge the romance of reading Italian stories while in Italy. It was books that had brought them together in the first place, after all. Sometimes they read to each other aloud in bed. As she narrowed her eyes and raised her hand to her forehead like a sailor to search through the strips of sunlight for him, Tasneem was reminded that this was one of the reasons she was so deeply attracted to him; she found she could speak to him of the words that moved her in a way that she had never been able to with anyone else, not without worrying about sounding pretentious, and certainly not with any of the boys her mother tried to introduce her to. Though they'd gone to different universities, they'd both studied English literature and would have graduated at the same time had Simon not decided to take his third year abroad. Sometimes, when she'd not seen him for a few days, she daydreamed about what it would have been like if they'd gone to the same university, lived in the same halls. She imagined sitting next to him in a lecture, the hairs on his forearm brushing hers. Suddenly, in the square, she was impatient to find him and in that moment, more than anything, all she wanted was to run into his arms and say, 'Look! Look what I found!' But she could not see him anywhere. The market was busier, noisier now. The lighter afternoon air had drawn even more people out from their air-conditioned holiday lets and a small pale blue truck had pulled up and was selling gelato. The cafés edging the square were filling up. She could hear live music playing, a woman singing an Ella Fitzgerald song. Still, she could not see Simon.

She paced the square for what felt like an hour although it was more likely half. She had pulled out her phone numerous times only to find no signal. She held her hand up to shade her eyes from the slant of the afternoon shafts of sun and scanned the square once more. She hesitated when she caught sight of the flash of Simon's mother's bright blond hair, bobbing up and down as she talked. There they were, the three of them sat at a small bistro table on bentwood chairs so delicate, Simon's father looked uncomfortable. The café was just out of view in the corner and so Tasneem had not noticed them sooner. She approached and then stopped for a moment, watching them so absorbed in conversation, a mother and a father both besotted with their only son, who held court as though he were a prince, Tasneem felt as though she ought to leave them alone, this perfect family so unlike her own. But then she also felt mildly appalled, because his parents were not even supposed to have been here.

His mother had phoned at the last minute. 'We're at a loose end,' she had said to Simon. She asked if they might tag along. What could Tasneem say, when it was their summer house in the first place, their son she was falling in love with? So when Simon asked her what she thought, she said it was a wonderful idea, that it would be a pleasure to spend more time with his parents, whom she had only briefly met once before. She clutched the book of short stories close to her chest and suddenly, she felt flat. All the fizz of sweet excitement and the girlish anticipation she'd felt just moments before, the urgency to show the book she had bought to Simon, to share the treasure she had unearthed, vanished.

'I asked you to wait,' she said.

He turned around. 'There you are!'

'I asked you to wait.'

'I did. But then you were a little longer than you said you'd be and we thought we might grab a coffee so...' He gestured at the thick mugs on the table, muddied pools of shiny dark coffee peering up from inside.

Simon's mother smiled at her and then tilted her head towards Simon's father and raised her eyebrows a touch as if to say, *lovers' tiff.*

'But I've been looking for you everywhere.'

'Okay, I'm sorry, Tas.' Simon stood up and talked slowly. He pulled over an extra chair. 'Let's get you a cold drink, and then we'll head back home. We bought fresh gnocchi for dinner. I thought you'd like it.'

She felt it then. Their sets of pale grey eyes upon her, innocent and uncomprehending small moons. There it was, the space wide between them. Simon and his parents on one side, and then her on the other. She knew then that it would always be there, this unspoken shore of misunderstanding, this vanity of small differences. The distance that made life so effortless, so easy, for Simon, so that he might take her on holiday with his wealthy parents to their elegant summer house and have her sleep in his flat three times a week, while she had to pretend to her own parents that he did not exist at all. The sort of misunderstanding that meant his father would mistakenly refer to her background as Indian instead of Pakistani or that his mother would continually place the emphasis of her name in the wrong place.

But then a wave of remorse washed weakly over her. Simon loved her, he had brought her to this beautiful place with its faded buildings and sun-drenched fields after all. She set the book of short stories down on the table and sat next to him, touched his knee, then pressed her palms into her face. 'I'm so sorry,' she sighed to all three of them, embarrassed. 'I don't know what's come over me. I'm all out of sorts.'

'It's only the weather,' Simon said, rubbing her back. 'It bothers you, that's all.' His mother made a sad-looking face and said, 'Poor thing.'

*

After dinner in the garden, plates of creamy gnocchi, Tasneem went up to bed early again. She hung back for a little while at the table, Simon's thumb lightly touching her wrist or else stroking the small of her back as he leaned legs-outstretched in his chair. When the conversation turned to one cousin's wedding and another's divorce, Tasneem took her cue to leave and said goodnight. Simon didn't press her to stay, didn't say sweetly, 'Sit with me for longer,' or 'I'll come to bed soon,' like he did when she'd yawn on his sofa and say, 'I think it's bed for me.' But she didn't mind quite as much as she had done the nights before because ever since they had returned from the market, Simon had been attentive to her. She had offered to help with the cooking but he rubbed her shoulders and brought her a glass of wine and said, 'No, stay, read your book – we've got it all under control,' and all through dinner, which they ate outside under the stars at the garden table lit by citronella candles, he squeezed her knee or touched her arm, her shoulder, her thigh; and so in this way, she felt they were connected again. Upstairs, she looked for the book she had bought but couldn't find it anywhere in their room. She realised then that she must have left it outside in the garden, where she had first started reading it, but she didn't quite have the energy to go all the way back downstairs and smile at Simon's parents just to retrieve it. Simon would bring it in anyway, she thought, as she fell asleep.

Later, in the middle of the night, Tasneem woke startled as a wild thunder ripped the sky apart. A storm had not been mentioned in any of the weather reports Simon and his parents read aloud to each other every day. She sat up in bed and looked over at Simon, his breathing deep and oblivious, his skin luminous in the moonlight. She didn't know when he'd come in or how long he'd stayed outside, drinking wine with his parents. She hadn't heard him open the door, hadn't felt him slide into bed. He hadn't reached for her waist or kissed her shoulder, hadn't tried to rouse her deliciously from her sleep. Tasneem walked over to the window. The night sky was mottled lavender and mauve, and the winds thrashed recklessly. Something pale flickered dully on the garden table, like a creature with a broken wing. She peered down and then realised what it was: the book she had bought from the market, blown open by the wind, rain splattering the pages like hard little stones; and just then she felt her heart dip like a moth falling away from a bright light. But the book would have to wait. It was not as though she could run into the garden in the silk lingerie she'd bought especially for this holiday, in the middle of this storm. It was not the end of the world. Perhaps the pages would dry out and even if not, she could easily buy another copy if she really wanted to, she could order one right now on her phone, and have it waiting for her as soon as she got home, but still she felt for a moment a strange sensation not unlike the surprise of a small but painful sliver of a paper cut. 'He didn't think to bring it in?' she thought, that was all.

Tasneem looked up. She noticed how the sky here so high up in the hills looked frightening, how it seemed deeper and denser than back home. Somewhere behind the hills, she heard the echo of stray dogs barking, savage and fierce. She glanced back towards the bed where Simon slept deeply, the pattern of his breathing steady, unaware of the emptiness beside him. She turned back to the window. In a few days, they would return home. They had not discussed their plans for after the holiday or for the rest of the summer. She wondered if he'd just expect her to go back to his, after they landed back in London, without necessarily asking if she even wanted to. She wondered how he'd react, if she made up some excuse about needing to go back to hers instead and do her laundry. She imagined he'd just say: 'Sure, that's fine, see you soon then,' and they would part with the briefest of hugs or the most perfunctory kiss, and that would be it. She could just picture him, saying that, doing that, as if it was nothing; assuming everything was fine. But all she really wanted was for him to insist, for him to tell her how unbearable it would be, to be separated from her for even just one night. She wanted only for him to make her feel like they were worth-while. Tasneem felt her breath catch at the back of her throat. She shuddered. She looked up and noticed how vast the space was between each lonely star, far apart distant planets vanishing behind the inky clouds and the endless dark.

# The Wishes

We told ourselves, Amir and I, that it was our third time lucky. We told each other this through quiet ultrasounds where I held my breath, waiting, studying the sonographer's serious face for clues, and we told each other this through draining blood tests that left me dizzy, my bright smile refusing to betray the edge of my fear. I told myself this, even as I felt the sharpness of the first signs of bloodshed and tried to convince myself it wasn't happening again.

Third time unlucky, I guess.

The third time was the worst time because it was also the best time and the longest time. My belly was swollen, plumper than it had ever been before, and my cheeks flushed in a way that made me stop a second longer at the mirror, a way that almost made me seem pretty. I sat at my writing desk, my palms criss-crossed over the tiny child fighting inside of me, its sporadic kicks flickering through me like a secret code that only the two of us understood. Sometimes I sat like this for whole mornings at a time, my hands kneading through the tight skin of my stretched stomach, searching for the vague bump of a fragile heel or the potential point of a tiny elbow just to remind myself that it was all real, this creature inside of me, that I had not just imagined it all. Those mornings, it felt as though we might just make it through.

When they told us our baby was small but growing well, we believed the worst of it was over. We were safe; nothing could go wrong at twelve weeks. We believed we were untouchable then. We cried and we laughed and we kissed like newly-weds. I touched Amir's face with the palm of my hand and it felt like the sun was shining just on us, a shaft of warm gold upon our skin. We went home, ate dinner in our pyjamas like excited schoolchildren on a sleepover and Amir rubbed my rounded stomach with so much sweet almond cream, I smelt like dessert. But then one week later she too was gone, a knife twisted in my side. I was empty again.

The third time was the worst time because I thought we would be okay.

*

For the longest time, I was not even sure I wanted children. It was expected of us, after eight years of marriage. Amir's mother always liked to ask when we would start trying, a term I personally found crude, but I was not sure I wanted it enough. I look back now and I want to shake myself. I want to say, do not think so long about what you cannot plan for. Do not take so long. Do it. Do it anyway.

Back then Amir understood. He felt the same way. Our friends had taken to moving out of north

London into commuter towns where the roads were wider and the parks greener, acquiring newly built houses with crayon-coloured gardens, driveways to park the big cars in which they planned to cart their tiny new babies around. But it felt remote to me. Not just the places, the towns they picked for their train links, but the idea of starting a family. It didn't feel like us, not yet. It was never the right time. I had seen too many friends, colleagues from the magazine publishers where I used to work, eventually turn freelance and then disappear after their babies turned a certain age. I had worked so hard on my books, I couldn't let that happen to me.

It wasn't just about work though. If I thought about it for too long, I realised that what I was most afraid of was being stuck and unable to escape, eventually turning bitter then resentful. My mother died when I was five and though my father had tried his best, it worried me that I might die young like my mother and leave a child behind, bereft of something they might never fully comprehend. I didn't tell Amir this.

But then something inside me began to shift like a cloud moving across the sky, only slower than the spin of the earth, and it left me feeling off kilter, out of place. I still cannot exactly pinpoint it but a few weeks before my thirty-sixth birthday, when the news of another friend's pregnancy was announced online alongside a blurry photo of a shape inside her womb, something within me turned. Later I blamed PMS when Amir asked what was wrong.

*

After the third time, I sat in the garden of our basement flat. Or rather, Amir carried me out there, as if I were an elderly woman in a care home, wearing bed socks in summer, smelling stale and dry. We did this every day for a while. He carried me under the shower. He carried me into bed. He carried the weight of me, the shell of what was left. But then Amir had to go back to work and I had to do something.

Except I did not. Months passed. I didn't write at all. Deadlines came and went; they didn't matter to me any more. Most days I didn't even leave the flat. Amir stopped carrying me; I had to get up, he said. But I didn't. I just lay in bed all day; it was literally all I did. I was aware that I smelt bad and needed to shower and wash my hair but somehow nothing seemed necessary any more. In the evenings, Amir started bringing dinner to our bedroom for me to eat but I turned away and ignored him. I ate when he wasn't home, because it meant that I didn't have to see him, that he didn't have to see me, and so every day, when he left for work, I crept into the kitchen like a crazed, hungry thief, eating cereal for breakfast and lunch and leaving the bowls unwashed, stacked in the sink. But then Amir started to forget to pick up groceries on purpose to draw me out, like some small captive animal, and I hated him for it. It was on one of those days, when I was hungry and angry and drawn out of my shelter, that I first saw it: the first crane.

On any other day, to any other person, it would have been rubbish tossed to the side, a flash of gold card fallen from the sticky hands of some small child carrying their art project home. But I noticed it because in those watery days, with my heart broken and my insides raw and spilt, I walked with the weight of loss and it made my head hang heavy and low. So that's how I came to notice it on the side of the pavement, this tiny little paper crane, and I swear, for a second, I saw it flit like a butterfly. I knelt down, picked it up by one wing and placed it in my palm. It twitched in the wind, as though it wanted to fly.

I must have mostly forgotten all about it until one afternoon when my father stopped by unannounced, something Amir had asked him to do. These little visits were insignificant in many ways, for all we did was drink tea and watch daytime TV or the news and sometimes he watered the garden for me, but they still meant something to me, and to him too, I think. I took something from sitting in silence with him on the sofa, unsaid words hanging in the air between us like particles. When my mother died it was what we did for years. I didn't need him to say anything. It was enough that he was there. I was a child once more, having lost the closest chance I had come to having my own. My father noticed the tiny crane sitting on my desk and picked it up, turning it this way and that in his hands, and then he laughed a little to himself, scratched his head.

'Your uncle and I used to make these when I was a boy,' he said. 'We used to drop them from the rooftop and watch them fly.'

'To their death,' I said. He ignored me.

'Fold a thousand of them, they say your wishes come true,' he said. 'That's why we used to do it.'

I guess I rolled my eyes. It was familiar to me, the ancient Japanese legend about the paper cranes, but familiar in the way of red roses and chocolates; a silly, spent cliché. After he left, I was about to throw the damn thing away, but then I wondered for a moment what I might wish for. Then I shook my head at the very absurdity of it.

But I suppose I needed something to do. I suppose my hands needed something to search for, something to hold onto. I suppose, having lost all the little people inside of me, having nothing left within me, I had lost my faith too. I could see little difference between praying to a God I wasn't even sure I believed in any more to holding onto some fairytale myth about paper birds making your dreams come true. I suppose I was broken. I needed something, anything, to stitch me back together again.

So that is how this all started. The folding, the paper, the birds. The wishes.

*

After my thirty-sixth birthday, something had started to shift. Our first niece was born. It was a cold week in April, the sun sliding out but not yet warm, the pale blossoms still folded inwards upon the trees. As I have said, most of our friends had already had babies and so it was not as though I had never held a newborn before. But when I first held Lana, she felt like stolen treasure. She was furrowed and fragile, only days old, with lips opening and closing as pink and perfect as the inside of a seashell. When I held her tiny weight, I felt an unexpected tug of something milky and warm, a longing, a reluctance to pass her along to Amir for his turn to hold.

Lana is older now, a firework exploding in all directions, but in those days I held her for hours, tracing the downy hairs that gathered on her forehead with my little finger. I noticed how Lana nestled neatly into the space between her mother's neck and her shoulder, how she fitted so perfectly there as though that were the only place she belonged. I remembered how my sister-in-law kept touching her absently all the while, her hand stroking her hair, her face, her foot. It startled me somehow. Had I never noticed this before with all of our friends, all of their babies? Surely, it had always been there. But then one night, unable to sleep, I realised what it was and I caught my breath in the dark. It was love. I understood that much now, but a different kind of love to what I felt for Amir. It was a love that felt out of reach and that was when I realised I wanted it for myself.

*

And so, three years later, it had come to this. I had one thousand paper cranes to make, yet over the course of an entire afternoon I had not even managed to make one. It irritated me that it took me so long to figure out the folds that a schoolchild had been able to make. I searched for instructions, easy enough to find online, but still, the squares and triangles and arrows that were supposed to show me which way to fold made little sense. I was fed up. As a writer, I sometimes had a way with words, but measurements and precision have never meant anything to me.

Amir returned home that day to an unexpected scene. I sat cross-legged on the living room floor, surrounded by paper scrunched up and scattered like discarded love letters, a pair of scissors held wildly in my hands. At first he thought I was cutting up my writing notebooks so he rushed over to me, but I reached out and hit his lower leg to stop him from stepping into my frantic domain.

I explained it in a rush, looking up at him. I told him about the legend and how it could bring me good luck, bring us good luck, and how if I could just make one thousand cranes it might mean, well, that next time we would be okay. We would be okay. I said this all, talking non-stop, the words just rushing out in a way that made me think that maybe I believed them. Scraps of paper stuck to my cardigan and my hair, and Amir looked down at me. And then he sat down, and studied the instructions in front of me as if, of course, it all made perfect sense, as if he too believed that a thousand paper cranes could bring a baby to life.

Amir, who possesses skills I do not, showed me how to make the cranes efficiently, his hands turning and smoothing the paper like a tailor handling rare silk. He wanted to help, but I told him he could not. The legend said the wish would only come true if I made them all myself.

*

By the new year I had made three hundred and thirty cranes. I was disappointed. I had thought I could make a thousand, easily, in a month or so. It was not as if I had other things to do. But it took longer than I had thought it would; the folding, the measuring, making sure the corners matched up. The strangeness of it caught me by surprise sometimes and I often wondered what I was even doing.

Even now I keep finding the early ones that were not quite perfect in various places around our flat, bent paper birds stuffed down the side of the sofa or squashed under the weight of the refrigerator, wingless and twisted and cold. When I find them, I keep them. Even the imperfect ones that, back then, did not count for the final tally. They still count for me.

Each fold I made carried my hushed prayers to the imaginary creatures I was making: my wishes. I wished that I could do it better next time. That there would be a next time. I wished that I could have a baby who would be healthy and happy and well and would last. A baby that would transform into a child, strong-limbed and surviving, messy and magical. I wished that we would not have to go through the loss again. And though I did not wish to forget them, I also wished that my ghost babies, my lost milky babies, might stop haunting me with their murmurs of pain and their boundless forms. I wished that I could think of them as something else, snowflakes or flowers or stars, instead.

*

Amir and I began to skirt around each other at home. Where once I spent day after day in bed, refusing to acknowledge the trays of dinner or the endless cups of tea he carried to me, and shrugging off the hand he rested on my shoulder or jerking my head away whenever he reached to gently stroke my hair, something had started to change since the birds, since the wishes. Things began to get better and I begrudged his love less. We began to overlap in corners of the flat and perhaps I even began to seek him out myself. In the kitchen he cooked pasta and tossed big salads and passed on anecdotes or filled me in on the family get-togethers that he still went to, but which I'd been avoiding ever since the third time. I found myself gravitating towards his voice as I did the dishes or he wiped the crumbs off the counters, aware that something in all this felt familiar, like it used to. In the living room, we started to sit next to each other on the sofa and even though we let the sound of the television fill the space between us, his hand still reached for mine and began to gently pull me into his side and I let it, I let him, because it felt good. In the bedroom I no longer lay, heavy and worn, with my back to him and in time, we stopped sleeping in sadness. He no longer had to reach out forlornly for me in the darkness only to feel me pull away. Slowly I found my way back to him, and he to me.

Each night Amir would say, 'Coming to bed?' and I would nod while counting my creations, packing the good ones away carefully in a large cardboard box, resting one atop the other gently. I would carry the box into the spare room and set it down lightly in the dark, a final brush of my hand on the tips of their crisp white necks and their wings, as if to say goodnight, and Amir would hold the spare room door open for me or else wait for me at the end of the hallway, his finger on the switch ready to turn the light off for the night, and while he waited he never once looked at me as though I had lost my mind for doing any of this. We never normally did anything for Valentine's, even before, but this time around he left a white paper crane that he had made for me on my pillow. Inside he wrote shyly in small black writing, *We will get there.* My cranes began to make me feel if not happy then at least somewhere close to content, like a small woodland bird nesting quietly in a safe place.

*

I had made eight hundred and ten cranes, counting them off in pencil on a tally sheet I kept taped to the fridge. When my father came, he never offered to help; never acted as if what I was doing was strange. On his birthday, I held out a crane for him and though I felt silly for it, he reached out, took it, gently stroked my hair. He keeps this crane still, and it hangs from the ceiling on a fine thread where it turns in the draughts that whisper through the windows, like a solitary slow dancer hanging in mid-air.

By early summer, I had made nine hundred paper cranes. I had almost finished. We went on holiday to Rome, the first trip we had taken in over three years, and I took a pile of paper with me in our suitcase. I made them up in our hotel room, sat cross-legged in the middle of our king-size bed wrapped in crumpled sheets with Amir, next to me; on rickety tables in streetside cafés; while sitting on the edge of St Peter's Square. We left the extras all over, studding the city in pairs like lovers kissing. We left them hanging in the tall trees surrounding the Villa Borghese; floating in the Trevi Fountain; in the bar in Trastevere, where we danced and I threw my head back and laughed and laughed and laughed. Back home, I unpacked the cranes I'd brought home with me and smoothed out their suitcase crinkles; I added them to all the other ones waiting for me, nestled inside the cardboard box in the spare room. By the end of summer, I had made more than one thousand paper cranes. I was pregnant again.

*

For the longest time, not just after the third time but even after the first, I told myself it was all my fault. Amir hated it whenever I said this so I eventually stopped saying it out loud. But that is not to say that I didn't believe it because I still did. We had both left it too late, we had both at first thought it was not what we wanted, but in the end it was my body that had failed us. I began to consider the possibility that perhaps I was not meant for this other life, of having babies, raising small people. I knew nothing of it after all. I had lost my own mother, had no memory of how she looked at me or talked to me or picked me up after I had fallen, and so, in some twisted sort of logic, I concluded that because I had lost a mother, I could not be one either. I began to tell myself that was the way my story was supposed to go.

*

Sometimes I still dream about them. Not as much, but sometimes. In my dreams my half-formed babies swim. They are translucent like jellyfish, pale crescent-shaped shadows coming through where their eyebrows should be. Like jellyfish they are heartless and blood-less but they are covered in veins and they are alight. They are swimming then they are drowning, then they are drowning still.

*

My fingers are covered in thin paper cuts. They are barely visible, minuscule slivers, etched on my skin, but I still notice them. I catch sight of them when I hold him close to my chest, his tiny hot fingers grasping mine, his short fast breaths beating real and alive against my skin, the soft spot of his crown pulsing like an X that marks the spot saying here, here is my treasure. I notice them when he nestles his scrunched-up pink face into that soft space between my neck, my shoulder, the place where he was always meant to be, my finely-cut fingers curled around him as though clasping a beautiful shell. Some days my heart is so overcome, it is all I can do to look away from him. It is all I can do to just take a breath and to know that if I do, when I do, he won't just disappear.

Sometimes I stare at him and I think he must have come from magic; sometimes I think he was born from the wishes. These days my cranes are no longer caged in a cardboard box in the spare room. They are bound to each other with a thin thread and they are draped all around the walls, framing his cot. They hush him at night, with the quiet rustle of their paper folds.

# Acknowledgements

*Things We Do Not Tell The People We Love* would have remained a dream, an unseen document saved on my desktop, were it not for the following people:

Laurie Robertson, my agent at Peters, Fraser and Dunlop, who first saw something in my stories and made me believe in myself. Your calm disposition and steadfast confidence in me and my writing carries me through periods of self-doubt; thank you for always reading.

Francine Toon, my editor at Sceptre, who understood my stories, and whose gentle, intelligent and probing insight helped finesse them with such delicacy. I feel so lucky, to have been able to work with you. And of course, everyone behind the scenes at Sceptre who has worked tirelessly on my book and championed me; thank you.

I wrote these stories shyly and it took me an awful lot of courage to share them. Abby Parsons, my first reader, encouraged me to keep going and made me feel like my words meant something; thank you for such thoughtful feedback and for guidance on navigating the world of publishing. Thank you also to Bernardine Evaristo, Alexandra Pringle, Caroline Michel, Erica Wagner and everyone at *Harper's Bazaar* for believing in my strange little story, 'The Jam Maker', which opened so many doors for me.

This past year has been weird, living in a pandemic, but I'm grateful to all the writers and readers I've been able to connect with online. Our conversations have made the act of writing feel a little less lonely, as it can sometimes be.

I would not be able to write at all, were it not for a particular kind of support. My immense gratitude to Lily Freitas, whose lively energy and deeply loving care for my children allows me the time to write without worry and whose presence uplifts us all. I am also unfailingly appreciative of all the teachers in my children's lives who provided structure during lockdowns and homeschool, which happened again and again while I was trying to finish this book, and whose endless support and guidance enabled us parents to somehow keep going when it felt impossible.

As ever, I'm beyond grateful to my immediate Qureshi and Birch families and especially to my parents, Mazher and Nusret Qureshi, for raising me the way they did; for a bedroom full of books and a childhood full of stories; for encouragement and love.

None of this would have been possible without you, Richard. The words thank you hardly seem enough, but I do thank you, so very much. Sometimes, I feel like I'm lost in a crowded room but then I look up and catch your eye and that's when I know, it will be alright. I am glad that I can tell things to you.

Finally, to my three beautiful sons, Suffian, Sina and Jude. You make my life dizzyingly brighter, so much so that sometimes I have to shield my eyes. Sometimes I wish time didn't have to move so fast, so that we'd have all this forever. You are all, each of you, magic.